Best-Friend's Billionaire Daddy in Italy

Izzie Vee

Published by Izzie Vee, 2023.

Table of Contents

Best-Friend's Billionaire Daddy in Italy: Adults Erotic Sex Stories

Rough Off-Limits Dad, Older Man Younger Woman Instalove Novel
Steamy, Forced & Forbidden Romance[1]

Izzie Vee

Erotic & Forbidden

[2]

IZZIE VEE[3]

---

1. https://www.amazon.com/dp/B09VYKS91Y

2. https://www.amazon.com/
   s?k=izzie+vee&i=digital-text&crid=31LQJTEQYT2EE&sprefix=izzie+vee%2Cdigital-text%2
   C121&ref=nb_sb_noss

3. https://www.amazon.com/
   s?k=izzie+vee&i=digital-text&crid=31LQJTEQYT2EE&sprefix=izzie+vee%2Cdigital-text%2
   C121&ref=nb_sb_noss

Important Readers' Note

Happy greetings!
Go follow me on Amazon with only 2 quick clicks. CLICK **THE FOLLOW BUTTON**[1] below to be notified about my hot new releases weekly. Then it'll take you to my Amazon's author page, where *you'll need to click the follow button on amazon's site as well*. It's that simple! Two quick seconds and you're all done!

[2]

Thanks for joining and be ready to be notified about the hottest releases sent straight to your inbox. Cheers!

---

1. https://www.amazon.com/-/e/B09VZQM39S

2. https://www.amazon.com/-/e/B09VZQM39S

Chapter 1

"Adam, for heaven's sake, please tell me this is a joke."

On the other end of the phone, Adam, Laura's boyfriend, sighed, his breath coming hard and heavy in her ear. A passing woman brushed against her shoulder, and Laura realized she had come to a halt in the middle of the walkway. She moved to the side, taking her luggage with her.

"Laura, it's not a joke. It's over. I can't be with you anymore."

"You're breaking up with me?"

She could hear the tremor in her voice, but she didn't care how weak she sounded in that moment. This was an absolute shock – the last thing she expected to hear from her boyfriend of two years.

"Babe—"

"Don't babe me, Adam. I'm here standing in a fucking airport in a strange city, waiting for you to join me. How can you do this to me? To us?"

Again, he sighed. "It's not you, it's me, okay?"

"Oh, don't give me that cliché bullshit. I deserve a decent explanation. You planned a romantic vacation for us, booked the hotel, the flight, the tours—everything. Now you're leaving me?" The vibration in her voice had disappeared, replaced by a tinge of anger that made her drop her carry-on bag to the floor. "I need to know what's going on!"

An elderly man looked up from his book, giving her a puzzled stare. She turned her back, running her fingers through her thick locks. "Fuck!"

She didn't find it strange when Adam changed his flight details at the last minute, telling her he would join her in Rome instead. His

5

excuse of having to urgently meet with a client made perfect sense; after all, he was a junior in his father's high-end investment firm whose eight-figure clients demanded attention around the clock. But she should have known something was off when she couldn't reach him on his cell phone all day, not until she landed in Rome and sent him a text message to let him know she had landed. It was as if he wanted her on the other side of the world before he delivered the terrible blow.

"It just wasn't working out, Laura. I didn't know how to tell you, but... I'm sorry. You need to move on."

He sounded so cold and distant, a far cry from the guy who swept her off her feet when they first met. Hell. Two years wasted on the man she thought was her soulmate, the would-be father of her kids.

As Adam spoke, Laura stood dumbfounded, trying to grasp his words. It was as if time had stopped. Nothing felt real. Slowly, her mind grasped the reality of the worst trip she had ever taken in her life. *What the hell should I do now?*

"I'll see you around, Laura. I never meant to hurt you, I swear," Adam said, the sadness clear in his voice.

It made no sense to Laura. If he was so unhappy about hurting her, why would he let her go? "Wait a minute, Adam. Talk to me. What's really going on?"

"I'm really sorry, Laura. I really am. But this is something I need to do."

"What you mean—"

Adam hung up, the click sounding like an explosion in her ears. It was over. Done. Instead of a romantic weekend with her boyfriend, she was now alone in a foreign country. It took a few seconds after he ended the call for Laura to snap back to her new reality. Surprisingly, her cheeks were still dry. It must have been the shock of the breakup that kept her from falling apart. Moving out of the terminal, she walked in a daze towards the exit and stopped where the taxis were parked, ready to take visitors wherever they needed to go. In her broken Italian, she instructed the driver to take her to the hotel Adam had booked for their stay. As the cab slipped into traffic, she leaned her head against the backseat and absorbed what had just happened. Slowly, very slowly, she began to thaw.

Oh, my God... Adam broke up with me!

A gentle sob escaped her lips, and she palmed her mouth to stifle the rest that threatened to rise. But she couldn't stop the tears. They fell in a rush, bathing her rosy cheeks. She and Adam had been happy, weren't they? Sure, they had issues like any other couple, and there were many little breaks in between, but they still had a good thing going, didn't they?

Why now? There were so many times he could have broken up with her, like when they had the terrible fight a few weeks ago about how distant he'd been or when she confronted him about his unwillingness to introduce her to his parents. No, he chose the worst time, when she was halfway around the world on a trip that was supposed to fix their relationship. She went overboard preparing for this trip. There was a dent in her savings to prepare for this romantic trip. She had placed a lot of effort in it too. She had ordered lingerie online and made trip to the upscale beauty shop her best friend Belinda recommended. She got her pubes waxed for him, for crying out loud! She wouldn't have endured that pain for any other man.

The taxi stopped in front of the hotel, and she checked into her room with a heavy heart. Seeing the king-sized bed with the beautiful towel swans, rose petals sprinkled all around, and the champagne chilling in the bucket brought home the heart-wrenching fact she would be sleeping alone tonight. She dropped her luggage and got to task, removing the decorations from the bed and dumping the champagne down the bathroom sink. After clearing every evidence of the romantic weekend she should have had, she sank down on the bed and succumbed to another round of tears that left her parched and weary.

She was still curled into a ball when her cell phone rang. Her heart skipped a beat and she kept her fingers crossed that it was Adam telling her he'd made a mistake. But it was Belinda, her voice so unnaturally chirpy it grated on Laura's nerves.

"I just got engaged!" Belinda shrieked, before Laura said a word.

"Oh, wow." The sudden tightening in Laura's chest made her take a deep breath. She curled her fingers around the phone and summoned a smile. "Congratulations."

Belinda seemed too wrapped up in her own news to notice the deadness in her best friend's voice. She went on about the proposal and the size of her diamond ring while Laura listened, the remains of her heart shattering into a million pieces.

"Ooh, my God, here I am harping about my engagement and cutting into your romantic weekend. We can talk when you get back, and I'm sure you'll have juicy details of your own!"

Laura took a deep breath. "Adam's not here. He broke up with me an hour ago."

There was a moment of silence on the other line, and then Belinda shouted, "Are you serious?"

"As a heart attack."

"Oh, my God, Sweetie. You must be devastated. What happened?"

Holding back the tears, Laura gave her a quick overview of the phone call at the airport, which left Belinda cursing on the other end.

"I can't believe he did that to you! What kind of asshole books a flight and hotel room, waits until you've flown halfway around the world, and *then* breaks up with you?"

Laura sniffed. "I don't know... it's just—I can't believe it. I don't understand how he could do this to me."

"And here I am going on and on about my engagement," Belinda sighed. "I feel horrible. I can't imagine what you're going through right now."

"Don't worry about it. I'll be okay." Laura bit her lip, wiping her stinging eyes. Her response was far from the truth, but 'fake it until you make it' was in full effect until she gathered the shattered pieces of her heart once more.

"What are you going to do now?"

"Well, I've got three days in Rome," she replied. "Might as well make the most of it, right?"

"Yes! That's the spirit!" Belinda's voice lightened. "Who knows, you might even meet a tall, dark, and handsome man who's going to sweep you off your feet!"

"That's the last thing I need right now." Just the thought of moving on made her want to hide under the covers. Adam promised her forever. How could she let that go?

"Oh, come on," her best friend insisted. "You're young, we are a few weeks from graduation, and now you're single! Make the most of it!"

"Belinda, I can't even think about another guy right now. Honestly. I just want to lick my wounds a little."

"Just as long as you're in good shape for my wedding."

"I'm sure I will be—"

"In June," Belinda finished.

"June? That's two months away!"

"I know. But Mom insists on a June wedding, and she refuses to wait an entire year."

Laura rolled her eyes, glad Belinda couldn't see her. She loved Belinda to death, but she couldn't stand her mom, Julie. The way she manipulated Belinda was too much for Laura to bear.

"Do *you* want a June wedding?" she asked.

"It doesn't matter. Mom knows best. I trust her."

It was a losing battle. There was no use trying to convince Belinda to grow a backbone and stand up to her mom. "As long as you're happy."

"I am." Belinda squealed. "I'm really excited, Laura, and I'm so looking forward to our engagement party next week."

"Already? But you guys just got—" What was she saying? Belinda was always looking for a reason to throw a party, and this was the most perfect excuse of them all. "Never mind. I'll be there."

"Awesome! Now, I don't want you wallowing in your hotel room for the entire trip, okay? Go out and have some fun."

"I will. Promise."

"I'm really sorry this happened, Laura. To say it sucks is a major understatement."

"It's fine, don't worry about it. And I'm really happy for you guys..."

And Laura meant it. Belinda and Henry had always inspired Laura since they hooked up in their freshman year. While most couples didn't last the test of time, they made it. There was no one more deserving of this awesome milestone. Tucking thoughts of her failed relationship aside, she leaned against the headboard and listened as Belinda talked about how Henry proposed to her.

"And oh, my God, he took me to this luxury restaurant overlooking the city..."

"I'm really happy for you, Belinda," she said when Belinda finally finished. "You are going to be such a beautiful bride."

"I know, right?" Belinda replied, giggling. "Mom has already gotten me an appointment at Kleinfeld and The Mews, and those are just the first two. I can't wait to try on wedding gowns. Aah!"

As supportive as Laura wanted to be, there was only so much she could handle about Belinda's big day. The heaviness had returned, and the green-eyed monster had started rearing its ugly head. She couldn't help wishing this was her happy ending, that the man of her dreams had swept her off her feet. Life was so unfair. All her life, she was always left on the losing side.

Why can't I win, for once?

"You okay?" Belinda asked, her voice tentative.

"I need to go, Belinda. The hotel needs to change my booking details since Adam's not here with me." The front desk clerk had already taken care of things, but Belinda didn't need to know that. She just had to get her best friend off the line.

"Oh, it's no problem." Belinda seemed to take the hint. "Are you sure you'll be alright?"

"Yeah, I'll be fine."

"Okay. I'll see you then. I'm really sorry about this, Laura. Message me when you're ready to talk!"

"Yeah, I will. Congratulations again."

Laura dropped the phone beside her and let herself fall against the pillows. A wave of exhaustion washed over her, reminding her she hadn't slept in twenty hours. The excitement of the trip had robbed her of sleep last night, and she had gotten up at the crack of dawn to catch her flight. Gone was the excitement, the happiness. In its place was the overwhelming urge to cry her eyes out. She closed her eyes and tried to sleep, but it would not come. There was too much on her mind.

The world has such ironic timing. Just when I got dumped, my best friend gets engaged, Laura thought.

She was happy for Belinda, but she couldn't help but notice how everyone was on a clear trajectory to accomplishing their goals while she had just been regulated to the starting blocks. She was always the odd one out, the broke friend, never being good enough to fit in. Meeting Adam had changed that reality for a while, introducing her to a whole new world, the side she'd only seen in the movies. Now that they were over, she imagined how things would change on that end. Not that she minded; she had never been comfortable in that world.

Removing her foggy glasses, Laura wiped them with the hem of her sweater. The honking of a car horn pulled her attention to the blue sky outside her hotel window and the wonderful Italian cityscape. It had always been her dream, especially as an art history lover, to visit the birthplace of Western art—well, in her opinion, anyway. If it weren't for this miserable breakup, she and Adam would have been strolling the streets right now, joining a sketching class or tasting the local cuisine.

I have to stop thinking about him. He's nothing but a complete jerk who's now out of my life. I should be thanking him. Didn't I dodge a bullet right there?

Belinda was right, of course. She had to make the best out of her trip. The breakup belonged in the past. Her endgame was to leave it there and focus on rebranding herself. No longer was she Adam's girlfriend, the girl whose social awkwardness his friends found 'cute' and 'different'. She would return to New York a new woman. A winner. Adam made the biggest mistake of his life, and she intended to show him.

The 'how' she would figure out soon, but for now, the regret on his face was enough to cheer her up a bit.

Wiping her face with the back of her hand, Laura got out of bed and headed to the bathroom for a shower. The afternoon lay ahead, and it was time to make the most of it. Staring at her reflection in the mirror, she ran her fingers through her damp hair, taking every inch of her body, running her palms over her tiny waist and her hips. This was a far cry from the size-twelve teenager she'd been, but the ghost of that insecure girl still lived inside her. Being with Adam had strengthened that flaw. She spent their entire relationship trying to prove she was good enough for him.

Two years wasted on a man who doesn't want me. How was I so blind?

Shaking off the moroseness, she got dressed, swapping her pair of glasses for the contact lenses she hardly wore because of how secure the spectacles made her feel. She applied light foundation and powder and just enough eyeshadow and mascara to accentuate her blue eyes. Adam hated it when she wore too much makeup. He said it looked fake and she was 'trying too hard'.

Fuck you and your opinion, you asshole. It felt liberating to apply the ruby-red lipstick that gave her lips a sensual look.

Satisfied with her appearance, Laura rifled through her luggage to find something suitable to wear. Because of the weather, she mostly packed sweaters and jeans, but the temperature was a balmy seventy-five, perfect for a dress. She chose a bright red sundress, one that clashed well with her pale skin. Slipping it on, she admired how it accentuated her curves without being too sexy. She twirled in front of the mirror, her auburn locks swinging before settling on her shoulders. Her mood improved a little, just a bit, enough to have her excited about exploring the city. As a finishing touch, she slipped on a pair of brown boots and dropped her sunglasses into a small cross-shoulder bag.

The sun kissed her skin, warming her insides and cheering her even more. She paused on the bottom step of the hotel, pondering where to go. To Adam's credit, he had chosen the best location in Rome, the epicenter of tourism. It was a little past midday, and the scent of food from the surrounding restaurants filled the air, whetting her appetite. She stopped by a cafe and bought an espresso and focaccia topped with fresh herbs and olive oil. After leaving the café, she headed to the first stop on her itinerary, a local art gallery where Adam had booked a drawing class with her favorite artist, Antonio Ricci. Despite her underlying bitterness towards her ex, she couldn't help being appreciative of the strings he pulled to make this happen. Maybe he did have a heart, after all.

But there was a 'closed' sign on the gallery door when she got there. Unable to believe her ex had pulled one over on her, she rang the doorbell, then tried peering through the tinted door.

"They're closed, signorina," a man said in passing, and she whirled around to face him.

"I saw the sign, but that's impossible. I have a class in ten minutes."

The man shrugged. "Maybe you got the dates mixed up." He gestured to a sign on the next door.

All live classes have been suspended until further notice.

Laura's heart sank when she read it. Yes, Adam had taken her for a ride. Add that to his list of sins. *I hope he burns in hell.*

Laura sighed and checked her itinerary for the rest of the day. There was no doubt the entire travel plan was worthless, so she threw it away, instead using the internet to find nearby landmarks. Her mood picked up when she realized the Trevi fountain was just a block away. On her way, she bought a cup of gelato and slipped on her sunglasses. She reached the fountain in no time and was immediately enthralled by the statue of Oceanus, his chariot being pulled by two sea horses and the cascading waterfall around them. The seats were already occupied, so she leaned against the wall, taking in the crowd-filled area.

There sure are a lot of couples here.

The bitterness returned, clenching her insides. Again, she wondered, *what's wrong with me? Am I the problem? Where the hell did we go wrong?* She was the perfect girlfriend—at least, she tried to be. It was no easy task, especially with a guy like Adam. Nothing she did was ever good enough for him.

Physically, he was the 'perfect' boyfriend. Tall, blond, handsome, and the heir to his father's prestigious investment firm. His charisma was just as prominent as his good looks, and his intelligence was also on par. Laura considered herself the luckiest girl in the world when he asked her out.

Back then, he was a college senior about to graduate. She was an awkward sophomore, just getting used to her new weight. Even now, two years later, she had no clue what he saw in her. Sure, people always complimented her beauty, but she never believed them. In her mind, she was a five on her good day. Adam was a ten. In fact, when they started dating, it shocked many of their peers on campus. By then, she and Belinda were getting closer, and she encouraged Laura to shut the haters out. Despite that, there was constant pressure to keep the flawless image going.

Laura wanted more than anything to be the perfect girlfriend, and she did everything in her power to change. Whatever Adam wanted, she catered to it. She cut back on carbs because he wanted a size two girlfriend. He couldn't stand the hair on her legs, so she endured waxing to keep them from growing back too often. His obnoxious friends were a pain in the ass, but she endured being around them for his sake.

Just thinking of the sacrifices made her pissed. *What do I get for enduring his shitty demands?*

"It's not you, it's me," he said.

Liar.

It's me. It's always been me. All the fighting, the ghosting for days… he was just giving her a preview of life without him. He had known for a long time what she knew now; she was never enough for him.

Her family wasn't from the upper class. They barely made the middle. They didn't own a brownstone in Manhattan, a villa in Miami, or a yacht in California. She hadn't stepped foot into a country club until she met Adam, and even then, she felt out of place. Hell, she couldn't have afforded this trip on her own.

Stupid, that's what I am. Blindsided. Naïve. I should have seen this coming. If I only realized what a tool he was, I could have saved myself the heartbreak. Instead, I clung to the first guy outside my league who had ever shown me any attention. Two years of my life wasted, trying to please a man who kept giving me empty promises.

The happy couples holding hands were a trigger, reminding her of what she lost. Moving away from the crowd, she found a quiet spot nearby. She dropped her bag on the seat, tears filling her eyes once more. She swallowed, her throat tightening. Burning. She clutched the base of her throat.

Something's wrong.

There was an irresistible urge to scratch her throat, but the action did nothing to soothe it. Her vision blurred, and her lips felt swollen. She glanced at her skin where red spots had appeared. A feeling of dread rose in her stomach when she realized the cause. She glanced at the cup of gelato she bought earlier.

Nuts!

Her throat locked, cutting off her air. Desperate, empty gasps left her mouth as she struggled to breathe. Her trembling hand released the gelato to the ground. She had been so distracted she forgot to tell the server of her allergy.

My EpiPen!

Laura dropped to the sidewalk, still gasping. Unfortunately, she was too weak to reach the bag on the seat. Giving up, she fell back against the pavement, her tear-filled eyes locked to the blue sky above.

Am I going to die like this?

A bulky figure loomed over her, blocking her view of the sky. The stranger reached down, giving her shoulder a gentle shake.

"Hey, miss, what's wrong?"

His deep, husky tone held a trace of alarm, but his expression appeared calm. Gasping, Laura pointed to her bag. The stranger immediately released her and rummaged through the bag. He found her EpiPen within a few seconds and injected it into her thigh. Laura sucked in a breath, her eyelids fluttering as her throat loosened.

"Hey... you're okay. That's it. Just breathe."

The stranger helped her to a sitting position, staring down at her with concern. Her vision cleared, and when she lifted her head to meet his gaze, a blast of self-awareness took over. There was a gorgeous man kneeling in front of her, a model straight from a Calvin Klein catalog. The salt-and-pepper sprinkle in his thick, dark hair gave him a mature look, but he had the body of a thirty-year-old. Her eyes roamed his muscular frame, taking in the brown leather jacket that hugged his broad shoulders and the biking gloves that covered his big hands. Was he a biker? She couldn't tell. Somehow, she doubted it.

"I'm calling an ambulance," he said, pulling out his phone.

"No need. I'm fine, really. The EpiPen worked."

The stranger shook his head, impatience lining his face. "No, you're not," he replied firmly. "Epinephrine is only a short-term solution. You need medical help right away."

Laura's eyes darted around her as a crowd circled them. Anxiety rose in her throat. Being the center of attention was never her thing, and she hated it even more now. She touched her cheek. Was it swollen? She couldn't tell. Her mascara-smeared hand confirmed how messy she looked.

There was a snicker, then another. Laura glanced at the crowd, searching for the source. *Are they laughing at me?*

A sudden wave of dizziness took over. She closed her eyes and took deep breaths, blocking out the spinning crowd. Memories of being teased in high school brought an overwhelming rush of anxiety that made it hard to breathe once more. This wasn't her first anxiety attack. In fact, it was a constant reaction whenever her vulnerability surfaced.

"I called the ambulance," the stranger said, gently stroking her cheek. "It's on its way. Breathe."

There was something about his touch that calmed her, and Laura could breathe once more. His piercing grey eyes searched her face, leaving a warmth that surprised her, considering the temperature had fallen. Laura struggled with the sudden, insane urge to touch him back.

This is crazy and so unlike me. I don't even know this man.

"There you go. Much, much better." The stranger smiled.

Laura's stomach flipped. *What's happening to me?*

Whatever it is, why do I like it so much?

Chapter 2

ELECTRIFYING.

The perfect description for the pair of big, blue eyes that flew open to meet Rob's gaze. They stood out in her small face, her brown hair framing her pale cheeks. Her lips parted as she gasped for air, clutching his wrist, the anxiety clear in her eyes. He stroked her cheek, and the action relaxed her shoulders. From the rosiness bathing her cheeks, she was obviously on the mend.

"Much, much better," Rob murmured, removing his hand from her cheek. It wasn't an easy feat. There was an urge to keep touching her. He didn't know why, but it felt good. Right. Insane. He had never experienced such a reaction to a woman he just met.

The crowd began to slip away. Reaching for her bag, Rob searched for an I.D. and found a passport in the small, zipped section.

Laura Turner. 23 years old. New York.

Laura. A beautiful name, just like the woman on the pavement. He helped her to a sitting position, and she groaned, triggering his concern. "Are you in pain?" he asked.

"I must have hit my lower back when I fell. It feels a little bruised." She arched her back, the action shifting his attention to the swell of her breasts, the creamy cleavage peeking over the semi-modest neckline of the dress she wore. The stirring of an erection took him by surprise. It had been ages since a woman had affected him like this.

She shivered a little, and he realized dark clouds had begun to form, and the temperature had fallen. A soft sigh escaped her lips as she wrapped her arms around her body.

Ignoring the flare of desire, he removed his leather jacket and placed it around her shoulders. She leaned against him with a gentle sigh, her soft body making him aware of how aroused he was. Her sweet, lavender scent didn't help either.

Fortunately, the ambulance arrived before his filthy thoughts grew worse. After using his fluency in Italian to inform the paramedics about Laura's condition, he watched as they carried her to the ambulance. A twinge of concern ran through him. This was a young woman, a tourist, who just had a near-death allergic reaction. She was probably all alone in this big city.

I should accompany her to the hospital to make sure everything's okay, right?

Ignoring the warning in his head, he made a split-second decision and joined her in the ambulance. She fell asleep as the vehicle made its way through the streets, and Rob took in her dozing form. Her face was slightly swollen, her eyelids puffy, but it didn't affect her beauty. This was a woman who could bring a man to his knees with just a curve of her finger. Perfect reason he should have walked away.

Damn it.

They arrived at the hospital, and he followed the paramedics as they wheeled her into the emergency room. They advised him to wait in the lobby, and again he questioned his decision to come. There was nothing else he could do for her. She was now in the best hands.

I should leave. Forget I ever met her. It's the sensible thing to do.

But he didn't. He took a seat in the lobby and distracted himself with a financial magazine from a nearby bookshelf. An hour passed before a doctor sought him out.

"You are Laura Turner's contact, yes?" she asked, and he nodded while getting to his feet.

"Is she okay?"

"She's fine. Luckily, you gave her that shot, or she would have been much worse."

"Great. Can I see her?"

"She's resting right now, so you may not get a response, but sure, you may see her." The doctor led the way to the hospital room down the hall. Laura lay propped against the pillows with one arm splayed across her stomach. She looked peaceful. The swelling in her face had reduced a bit. After handling the paperwork for her hospital bill, he took a seat by her bedside, watching her every moment and admiring her.

Half an hour later, Laura's eyelashes fluttered, and she shot up in the bed with a gasp.

"Hey... relax."

"Where am I?" she said with a moan.

"You're in a hospital," he informed her. "Don't worry, you're in great condition. Just a minor bruise from your fall, but it should clear in a few days. The doctor had already discharged you, but if you want an official review, I'll go get her."

"No, that's fine." She looked around the room, then back at him. "I didn't get your name."

"It's Robert. My friends call me Rob."

A tiny smile pulled at the corners of her lips. "I'm so sorry, Robert —"

"Rob."

"Rob, you didn't have to... you went through all that trouble—"

"It was no problem," he replied. Lies. It was a problem. She was already under his skin. A dangerous place for any woman to be.

"Thank you for saving my life."

Her mesmerizing eyes touched his soul, triggering a longing that made him uneasy. He looked away, unwilling to meet her gaze any longer. There was nothing else there for him to do. She was fine. He already paid the bill. Somehow, he found it hard to leave. There was something about her that drew him in, leaving an urge to know more about her.

Leave, asshole. She's obviously a decent girl. She doesn't deserve to be ruined by the likes of you.

He wished his conscience would just shut up, but he couldn't deny how right it was. Laura deserved a guy who could commit, not a man who only wanted to fuck around. He had no problem finding willing women with a similar aim. Time to walk away.

Pushing to his feet, he cleared his throat. "It was nice meeting you, Laura. Now that you're okay, I think I should go—"

"No!" Laura blurted, reaching for his arm.

His brows shot up, he glanced at where their bodies connected, and the instant surge of pleasure that ran through him sent blood rushing to his cock. If a single touch affected him this much, he couldn't imagine what would happen if—

No. Fuck no. I won't go there.

"I want to thank you properly," she said, a hint of red climbing up to her cheeks. "Let me at least buy you dinner. It's the least I can do."

"Um..."

Don't do it, Rob. Walk the fuck away.

He stared at her innocent face, realizing the biggest reason he had to say no. She was too young. His usual conquests were women in their thirties, experienced women who knew what they signed up for. Instead of turning her down, he said, "Sure, why not?"

Laura beamed, the sight warming his insides. Again, there was that overwhelming urge to touch her. Giving in to that longing, he reached down and helped her off the bed. It took every ounce of his willpower to let her go.

This is odd. We haven't even kissed or . Why does she affect me so much?

The sun was almost kissing the horizon when they left the hospital. He could sense her awkwardness as she wrapped his jacket around her shoulders to protect herself from the afternoon chill. He understood her reaction. He *was* just a complete stranger, even though he saved her life.

"Can you handle walking, or should I call a cab? I left my motorcycle at the fountain."

"Walking is fine. I need the fresh air, anyway."

The awkward silence continued as they walked on, heading toward a chain of restaurants on the tourist hip strip. Rob tried not to keep staring at her, but he couldn't help it. Her beauty compelled him to.

"So, how come you're touring this big old city alone?" he asked. It was a fishing expedition. He wanted to know if there was a man in her life. Not that it was important; he had no intention of crossing the line. But he was curious.

Dark clouds suddenly formed across her face, and she swallowed, staring down on the pavement. "Being alone wasn't part of my plans, believe me."

"What does that mean?"

"It's a long story," she replied. "My boyfriend - uh, ex-boyfriend, didn't come."

"Oh."

"And then I thought, 'Hey, why not make a big trip out of it?' So I went to a gallery, but it was closed, and then I went to the Trevi, and I almost died." She let out a laugh and shot him an apologetic face. "I'm sorry, you must think I'm ridiculous for blabbing my business to a stranger."

"Well, I did save your life," he joked. "I guess you can say I'm not a complete stranger."

A soft blush filled Laura's cheeks, and she licked her lips, directing his attention to them. Pink, plump and succulent. Did they taste as delicious as they looked?

One way to find out, Rob. You are never one not to pursue what you want, are you?

No, not with her. I've already decided to leave her alone.

"You're right," Laura said, yanking him from his thoughts. "Thank you very much again for saving my life. I guess my trip can't turn out much worse than today."

"For the last time, Laura, it was nothing. Happy to help."

The streets were filling up with people heading for the nightlife. The restaurants and shopping malls were buzzing with activity. This was exactly what he wanted; no privacy, no chance for him to succumb to the desire to seduce her.

"Where would you like to eat? I'm really not familiar with the city."

"Anywhere is fine," he replied, pointing to a bistro nearby. "How about that place? I hear they serve the best tiramisu."

Laura nodded, and they crossed the street to the small restaurant and took an outdoor table. Rob removed a cigarette from his pocket when they sat down.

"Is this okay?" he asked.

Laura nodded. "Sure, go ahead."

Rob lit up and offered the cigarette to her. There was a brief hesitation before she shrugged and said, "Why not?"

A rough cough escaped her lips when she took the first draw. Gasping, she handed it back to him.

Rob shook his head with a chuckle. "Something tells me you've never had one of these before."

"I haven't. Now I remember why," she replied, chuckling. "Add that to the list of things I will never try again."

"Care to share that list?"

"It's quite short. There's bungee jumping, eating octopus, getting my pubes waxed..."

Rob groaned inside. *I didn't need that visual, goddamnit.* Now he couldn't stop wondering if she was bare down there. "Why did you even try? You obviously hated doing them."

Her shoulders hunched with a casual shrug, but a flash of anger crossed her face. "I wanted to fit in."

"How did that work out for you?"

"Well, I'm all alone in Rome, aren't I?" she replied, spreading her arms. There was no missing the bitterness in her voice.

"Do you want to talk about it?"

"Nope." She waved to a server and ordered a slice of tiramisu.

"I'll just have an espresso," he told the server.

As soon as the young man left, Laura leaned towards him with both arms on the table, all trace of her irritation gone. "So, what are *you* doing in Rome?" She seemed genuinely interested, but he couldn't reveal the true reason for taking an impromptu trip halfway around the world. Instead, he gave her a watered-down version.

"I wanted a break from the business, so I took a week off to relax, do a little sightseeing. Nothing interesting, really," he said.

"Oh." She raised an eyebrow. "Where are you from?"

"Born and raised in New York."

"Are you kidding? I'm from New York!"

"I know," he replied. "Saw your passport."

Another reason he couldn't fuck around with her. New York was a big city, but it was too close to home.

"Where in New York are you from?" she asked.

He smiled. "It's my turn to ask a question. Why didn't your boyfriend come with you?"

"Ex-boyfriend," she clarified. "So, you're the one asking questions now?"

"How about this." He leaned towards her, and she wet her lips. "We'll take turns asking questions."

"Fine by me." She returned the smile.

"Why didn't your boyfriend come?"

Laura let out an exasperated sigh. "He broke up with me, just as I arrived at the airport. And that's the only discussion I'm having about it."

Rob nodded, understanding her need for privacy.

"Everything okay? He asked when he found her eyes on him.

"How old are you?" she asked.

He laughed. "Don't you know it's impolite to ask people about their age?"

"Well, that's not fair." She leaned against the back of the chair, crossing her arms. "Especially since you probably know more about me from snooping in my passport."

"I'm forty-four," he replied. "And I wasn't snooping. I needed information for the paramedics."

"Are you married?"

He laughed again. "You sure are curious, aren't you?"

"Of course, I'd like to know who I'm talking to." She grinned, sweeping her hair over her shoulder.

Rob sensed she was coming out of her shell. She seemed confident, witty, and undeniably attractive. Whoever broke up with her was a complete ass.

"Divorced. One kid. What about you?"

"Never married. No kids. Last year in university."

"Oh, what are you studying?"

Her face fell. "Finance, but I hate it. I wanted to study art history, but my mother refused to pay my tuition if I did. My passion is art. I want to manage my own gallery someday."

"Impressive. I'm sure you will do well."

Her smile illuminated her face. "Thank you. It means a lot."

The server interrupted their conversation when he brought the tiramisu and espresso. As Rob took a sip of his coffee, he cast another glance at Laura as she took a happy bite from her dessert. She licked her lips, and again he wondered about their taste. Again, he shook off the filthy thoughts.

Her eyes lifted to meet his, and she giggled. "What?"

"You're beautiful." The words left his mouth before he could stop them. He shook his head, ignoring the flutter of his pulse. For some reason, he wanted to keep that smile on her face. The warm, emotional rush surprised him.

What's happening to me? This is nothing but a physical attraction, right?

Deep down, he knew this was more than fire-hot chemistry between them. The realization made him nervous. He'd spent years building up the walls that kept him safe, now he was surprised to hear knocking coming from the outside.

"So, have you been on any tours since you got here?" Laura asked as she took another bite.

"I've done a few." He sipped his coffee, his eyes locking with hers. "I like riding alone, though. It helps me meditate. I like the feeling of the open road."

Her awesome expression remained in place as he told her about the places he'd been. France, Spain, and all the way to the Isle of Man. He found it cute the way she tried to understand the motorcycle jargon and how she listened keenly to all his stories. It surprised him how much he enjoyed their talk.

"It's so freaking cool that you own a motorcycle. I could use a little adventure," Laura said as he waved for the check.

Again, he ignored the warning bells and replied, "Why don't we go for a ride?"

Laura grinned. "I'd love to. Sounds like crazy fun."

After paying the bill, Rob escorted her from the restaurant, and they walked over to where he parked his motorcycle. He handed her his extra helmet and gunned the engine.

Laura let out a nervous laugh. "This is crazy. I can't believe I'm doing this." She climbed up behind him, her hands clutching his waist. Her scent washed over him, triggering another rush of desire that gave him an uncomfortable hard-on.

You and me both, Laura. "Grab tight," he said, pulling her arms around his torso. "Don't let go."

"I won't," she murmured near his ear, her soft voice sending a tingle down his spine.

His heart rate climbed as her warm body pressed against him. It was an agonizing ride, having her so close, her softness enveloping him. With the approaching nightfall in mind, they took a quick tour around the city. The sun had already set when he stopped by his favorite spot on Gianicolo Hill, where the beautiful view of the city lay beneath them.

"Oh, my God. This is the most breathtaking sight I've ever seen," Laura whispered, her dancing eyes glistening with awe.

I beg to differ, Rob thought, taking in the wonder on her face. The powerful urge to take her in his arms was almost too much to bear, so he backed away, giving her—and him, much needed space.

When Laura finally got enough of the view, they hopped on the bike again and toured the outskirts of the city. Rob cut his speed, wanting to extend his time with her. Night had already fallen when they arrived at Laura's hotel.

"So... I guess this is goodbye," he said when she alighted from the bike.

She handed him the helmet with a smile, sensuality bathing her features. "Does it need to be?"

A wiser man would have ended the conversation and gotten the heck out of there. Instead, he replied, "What do you have in mind?"

"I brought a few sketches with me. Would you like to see them?"

Laura's expression held no innocence. Her intentions were clear. *Say, no thanks Laura, start your engine and go. It's quite simple, Rob.*

"I'd love to." He offered her a smile.

Somehow, as they walked to the elevator, the atmosphere felt different. Gone was the awkwardness of this morning. At this point, it was if he'd known her forever. It was like the most natural thing seeing his jacket around her shoulders. She seemed relaxed while they rode the lift, but her fingers shook a little as she fumbled for her swipe card when they reached her floor.

"So, Rob," she said, opening the door to her room. "Welcome to my temporary abode."

It was a small hotel room, but with a spectacular view of the ocean through the floor-to-ceiling glass doors that led to the balcony outside. A queen-sized bed lay in the center with two nightstands on either side. There was a small pile of her clothes in the corner, and she tossed them into her suitcase with an embarrassed groan. Rob found it cute that she cared about his opinion of her.

"Um... have a seat... wherever I guess." She gestured to the couch, then the bed with a shrug. Leaning to the side of caution, Rob took the couch, his fingers making nervous beats on his knees while he waited. This was an unfamiliar emotion, this uneasiness. He hated how it made him feel.

"Here we go," Laura said behind him, appearing before him a second later with a satchel tucked under her arm. She took a deep breath and revealed the sketchpad underneath and hesitated before handing it to him.

"They're not that good, though," she said as he took it.

Rob examined the first sketch, his brow lifting as his fingers traced the exquisite urban art. "Not good? Are you kidding me? This is stunning. It takes a lot to impress me, and I am." He looked up at her, smiling. "You have quite an extraordinary skill."

"You're just saying that," she replied, a soft blush bathing her cheeks.

"I mean it, Laura. You're clearly shy about your work, but you have talent."

"You think so?"

"I know so."

"Thank you," she said. "Although Adam kept insisting I still need a lot of practice."

Oh, so that's the ex's name.

"Who cares what Adam says?" he scoffed. "These are amazing. They belong in a gallery."

The overwhelming gratitude in Laura's eyes made him pause flipping through the rest of the sketches. Placing the sketchpad on the seat, he got up from the couch. Her eyelashes fluttered as he approached her, and she took a step back.

"You don't get complimented often, do you?" he asked.

"Not really," she mumbled.

"Such a pity." She didn't flinch when he ran his fingers through her hair. "I guess no one told you how beautiful you are."

She shook her head, her mouth slightly parted, her soft breaths arousing him again. The sexual tension was so heavy and thick, there was no way to ignore it. Rob didn't want to, anyway. His primal instincts were on a high, pushing him to divide and conquer.

Muffling his conscience, his fingers traced down her cheek. Laura gasped softly when his thumb brushed her lips. "Juicy. So fucking... kissable."

Laura moaned, her eyes flicking shut. She wet her lips, and the silent invitation made him lean down, taking her mouth for a deep, hard kiss.

Chapter 3

IS THIS HAPPENING, or am I dreaming? Is Rob really kissing me? God, if this is a dream, please don't let me wake up. I couldn't bear reality after this heart-stopping kiss.

Rob palmed her ass, the gentle squeeze an exhilarating confirmation. It was real and so fucking good. Hard, hot, breathtaking, burning into her soul. This was a fantasy she never thought would come through. Rob was obviously attracted to her, but she sensed his reservations too. Whether it was their age gap, or the fact he was probably seeing someone else, she didn't know. Or care. He was the balm she needed for her wounded soul, if only for one night.

Laura looped her arms around his neck, inhaling his spicy scent with each stroke of her tongue. His hands made their way to her waist, gripping tight, pulling her against him. The rock-hard evidence of his arousal pressed against her stomach, sending a heatwave between her thighs. The ache for him intensified. She wanted him inside her so much.

Disappointment tore through her when Rob broke away with a sharp hiss, dragging his hands down his face. "Fuck, Laura. I shouldn't have done that."

"Done what, kissed me?"

"Everything." He sighed, creating distance between them. "I shouldn't have taken you out, stepped foot in your apartment, kissed you—"

"But I wanted it. Doesn't that count?"

There was a newfound confidence she'd never felt before, especially not with Adam. There was something about the way Rob looked at her as if she were the only woman in the world. It made her sexy, bold, ready to break from her shell.

"You don't know what you're asking of me," Rob said, the agony clear on his face.

"But I do," she whispered. "I want you inside me, Rob."

"Fuck," Rob mumbled, groaning.

She didn't want this night to end. She wanted him to stay. She wanted this one night with him, even if it would be the first and the last. "Please."

"Are you sure?"

"Positive. I've never been more certain of anything in my life."

Laura let out a small gasp as Rob lifted her, his lips capturing hers once more. She wrapped her legs around his waist, losing herself to the ecstasy his lips gave her. She had no doubt Rob could fuck. He kissed like a man who was skilled in bed. Her anticipation grew. The wait became unbearable.

"I need you to fuck me, Rob," she whispered against his mouth. "Now."

Rob growled in reply, moving her toward the bed. Her heart rate increased when he laid her down and removed his shirt. *Yes, definitely the body of a thirty-year-old,* she thought, taking in his sculpted torso. Oh, she wanted to touch every inch of his gorgeous frame.

Rising to her knees, she ran her hands over his stomach, confirming it was just as hard as it looked. Rob watched her, the arousal in his eyes making her bolder. She dipped and licked his nipples, satisfied when he let out a soft hiss. Her lips traveled upwards, tasting his skin, nibbling its way to his mouth. Rob gripped the back of her head as their lips touched once again. The spark that started at the pit of her stomach now turned into a blazing bonfire. She could feel the warmth of his body as his stomach pressed against hers. In the heat of the moment, she slipped her tongue inside his mouth. Rob accepted the invitation and met her tongue with his. He teased her skin, tracing the shape of her collarbone with his fingers, pulling down the straps of her dress. Her flesh turned pink from his touch. She dug her fingers into his back, urging him to undress her. Rob obliged and with their lips still intact, he unzipped her dress and pulled it off.

Laura let out a small moan as Rob's lips moved from her mouth down her neck. He expertly unclasped her bra and tossed it aside. His lips traced where his fingers had been before taking a nipple into his mouth. Laura was never vocal in bed, but Rob's sensual licking and nibbling on her nipple triggered sounds of pleasure she couldn't hold back.

Rob moved downwards, his lips leaving a hot trail as he made his way between her thighs. Laura gasped as he gripped the waist of her panties with his teeth and pulled it down her thighs and off her feet. She tossed her head back, her eyes rolling to the back of her head, her teeth clenching on her lower lip as he licked her inner thighs. She could feel the wetness in her center and the intense craving for more. But he kept teasing... driving her insane.

"Rob, please..." she moaned.

Rob chuckled, the sound vibrating between her legs. His warm breath bathed her thighs, traveling until his tongue met her craving sex. Laura cried out, her legs instinctively closing at the first lash of his hot tongue.

Rob looked up at her every now and then, though the sight of her soft, parting flesh was something that simply enthralled him. With every lick he made, his tongue moving between her slit, she quivered a little, followed by a moan that made him even more painfully hard. He couldn't get enough; couldn't get enough of her sweet flesh that reminded him of rain. Currently it was pouring and he was basking it all of it as he lapped up the juices she was spilling for him. Rob latched his mouth to her sensitive bud and suckled hard, enjoying the sounds of Laura's heightened moans. She gripped onto the sheets and snapped her eyes shut, pleasure swelling inside her as her body prepared itself to orgasm. She gave up, moaning and spasming under the intense pleasure of his tongue. She was on the verge of a climax when Rob paused, towering above her, a cocky grin on his face as he licked her juices off his lips.

Laura breathed heavily, her hands desperately clawing at him, her body jerking impatiently. "Don't stop. Please."

"Oh, Laura. I don't intend to stop. I'm just getting started," he murmured, his expression wicked. He unbuckled his belt and tossed his jeans aside. His boxers soon joined them. Laura pushed up to a sitting position on the bed, her eyes hazy as she took him in. He was huge, not what she was accustomed to. She wondered if he would fit as she stared at him in awe and a little bit of panic.

"Like what you see?" he murmured, stroking himself.

Laura licked her lips. "Very much."

He stepped closer, offering himself. "Take me in your mouth, Laura. Suck my cock."

With the fire raging inside, she got on all fours and licked the bulbous head with her ass propped in the air. Rob let out a satisfying moan when she slowly took his length in her mouth. He ran his fingers through her hair as she eased into a rhythm, feeling completely in control as he moaned with her every move.

"Yes Laura, deeper. Take every inch of my cock. I know you can... ugh, fuck, yes..."

Laura pushed further, taking him in, almost gagging when the tip hit the back of her throat. She held on, sucking vigorously until his thighs quivered, his mouth spewing the filthiest words she'd ever heard. His grip tightened around her hair. Laura pulled away, and he released out a loud groan.

"I'm only returning the favor," she said, grinning.

Rob scowled, pushing her back onto the bed positioning her on all fours, her tight ass like an offering. Trickles of her arousal dripped down her thighs. She gripped the sheet, moaning as her caressed her ass.

"So fucking gorgeous. I can't wait to see it bouncing as I take you from behind." He pressed inside her with a groan, his beefy length slipping past the soft folds of her waxed pussy. Laura cried out as he braced more of himself inside her, her walls stretching to accommodate him while her flesh clenched around him. She'd never been filled like this. Not even close.

"Ahh, nice and easy, baby. Fuck, you're tight," he said between clenched teeth.

Rob grabbed her hips, bucking into her and lunging his length to the hilt. Laura's broken moan filled the air, her body stiffening a little as she tried her best to relax. Rob bared his teeth and gripped her thighs tighter, pulling back a little before he plunged into her yet again. He moaned, his hands moving down her ass cheeks as he pried them apart and filled his gaze with the image of his cock driving back and forth inside her. He was glistening wet, his veiny cock completely stuffed inside her tight, little quim.

God help him.

Laura fully submitted to his hard strokes, doing her best to cling onto whatever control she had left. He picked up the pace, drilling her. Laura could feel every inch of him as he moved inside her, filling her in places she never knew existed. Her mouth hung open and after a few more unforgiving strokes, she licked the saliva that had trailed down her lips and began to moan again.

She let out loud, rhythmic moans of pleasure, her grip tightening around the sheet. He grabbed her arms and pulled her towards him with her back touching his chest. He sank deeper and the breath hitched in her throat as she experienced a bittersweet mix of pain and pleasure. She jolted, her body shaking with ecstasy. Heavy breaths escaped her lips. She wouldn't last much longer. Rob kept stroking deep and hard, moaning into her neck with one hand fully clasped around her left breast. The distribution of pleasure made Laura shudder; her body was a melting pot of pleasure and every touch ignited more arousal within her.

Rob moved his other hand down in front of her and rubbed his fingers over her swollen clit. Laura gasped, her pussy tightening around him instantly. Rob continued, feeling a new rush of juices that hugged his cock as he moved inside her. As he thrashed his fingers on her clit, he realized she got even wetter than she was before. Somehow that invigorated him, his manhood slipping back and forth inside her with more ease. Fireworks sparked along her spine with every movement of his fingers on her clit and Laura's eyes rolled over in the back of her head, her mouth agape.

"Don't stop..." she moaned.

Rob let out a grunt as her tight ass smacked against his hips. His rough grunts betrayed how close to the edge he was. Laura's sex gripped him, pulsing. There was no holding back any longer. With several thrusts, he finally let go. Laura's body trembled as she fell over the edge, joining him on the ecstatic cloud that floated to the bottom. His hot release filled her, spilling deep inside her. His hands still palmed her breasts, gripping them, clearly with no intention to let go. Their heavy, rhythmic breaths filled the room, the warm sweat trailing down their bodies. Even after he emptied himself inside her, Laura continued to grip him until his manhood became flaccid. Rob pulled out, a trail of his hot cum slithered out from her, a dollop dropping to the bed. Both dropped to the bed with an exhausted sigh.

No more words were said that night. Laura curled into him, and the only thought on her mind was the absolute bliss of having him near her. It felt natural. Right.

God, I need more than one night with this man.

WHEN LAURA AWOKE, THE scent of the ocean hung heavily in the air, bringing her attention to the open balcony door. Easing out of bed, she slipped on a T-shirt lying on the floor. As she closed the window, a soft moan from behind made her turn around. She stared at the muscular figure sleeping under her sheets, and a blush crept onto her face. Rob was obviously still in dreamland as he laid on his back on *her* bed with the sheet covering his lower half, his tousled hair, his slightly parted lips, and his gorgeous abs on display.

This is the perfect sight to wake up to this morning. What more could a girl ask for?

Sinking into a nearby armchair, Laura reflected on the day before. What should have been a romantic reconnection had turned into disaster, but Rob saved the day. Her fingertips grazed over her lips as memories of last night took over. She could almost feel Rob's tongue between her thighs, licking her clit, his cock touching her sensitive spot. Those fingers should come with a warning sign: *Dangerous*. A spasm of pleasure ran through her. Was it possible to be addicted to someone so soon?

She curled up on the seat, watching him, taking in how sexy his salt-and pepper hair made him look. She'd never been with an older man before.

Especially a stranger.

Oh, my God. What did I do?

Laura buried her face in her hand, sighing. The age gap wasn't the only complication to their situation. What if he lied about being divorced, and he was still married with kids? There was no wedding ring on his finger, but that meant nothing these days.

Her chest tightened with the onslaught of another panic attack, and she took deep breaths to remain calm. This was nothing but her defense mechanism chipping in. Last night was perfectly natural. Sex between two hot-blooded consenting adults. Definitely not an act she should be ashamed about. She was in Rome, one of the most romantic places on Earth, with a tall, handsome, middle-aged biker from whose pores dripped panty-dropping charm. She had been dumped, lonely, and vulnerable, and he arrived just in time to literally rescue her, just like a knight in a shining leather jacket. It was only natural for her to want him, right? It didn't help the fact that he wanted her too.

Another groan came from the bed and caught her in mid-thought. Rob was still asleep, his back now turned to her, giving her a generous view of a dragon tattoo she missed last night. She moved to the bed, inspecting, tracing the intricate details.

Rob's head suddenly twisted, his sleepy eyes meeting hers. "Enjoying the view?" he asked, the sexy huskiness sending a tingle up Laura's spine.

She gave him a weak smile as he ran a hand through his hair and pushed to a sitting position. Self-awareness took over. Here she was, dressed in a thin T-shirt with no panties, and he was obviously very naked under the sheets.

He got out of bed, and Laura's eyes dropped as the covering slipped from his body, revealing his hard cock. Arousal swirled in her stomach, sending heat between her thighs. She licked her lips as he approached, already tasting him on her tongue.

"I enjoyed last night." Rob smiled, leaning over to kiss her neck. Laura blushed, at loss for words.

"What happened to the sexy vixen I was with last night?" he asked, his eyes locked to her lips.

"She's still hibernating, I guess."

Rob scoffed, his gaze dipping. He reached out and grabbed the hem of his T-shirt. "This looks so much sexier on you than me," he murmured. "But I'd like it back, please."

"What if I don't want to return it?" She bit her lower tip, twisting her body seductively. "I love how it feels on me."

Rob sighed as she backed away from him, his eyes darkening. "Take off my shirt, Laura."

"Make me." Her new confidence was a pleasant surprise. She liked this new version around him. A completely new person. For some reason, the cosmos were giving her a do-over.

He grinned. "I do love a challenge."

Laura's smile dwindled as he drew closer. She sucked in a breath when his fingers brushed her thighs, moving upwards. Her sex throbbed, aching for his touch. A soft moan left her lips when he grazed the seam of her flesh in a slow, teasing motion. He pressed his fingers inside, gliding with ease and looking deep within her eyes as he did it. Laura's mouth fell open as he curled his fingers inside her and pressed his forehead to hers.

"Fuck..." Rob exclaimed, unbridled lust on his face. "You're so fucking wet. So ready for me."

"Yes," Laura breathed, moving her head just a little so her lips grazed his. She rocked her hips, meeting his torturous thrusts. Heat blossomed in her stomach, spreading to every inch of her body, leaving her with a desperate need for release. His fingers were good, giving her insurmountable pleasure, but she wanted the rock-hard thrusts from his cock.

"I need you inside me, Rob," she whispered, blushing from her boldness. This wasn't the time for brashness. She wanted to come.

A flash of mischief crossed Rob's face before he murmured, "And *I* need you to return my shirt."

Laura gasped as he removed his fingers. Her body quivered from the sudden loss. "You're cruel."

"You're still wearing my shirt."

She huffed, lifting the hem and hauling it over her head. Her eyes met his lustful stare. He licked his lips, closing the gap once more. "Much better," he said, dragging his wet fingers across her lips. He pried them further apart before he slowly slipped them inside her warm mouth, willing her to suck herself from his digits. Laura caught them into her mouth and sucked hard, moaning a little as she stared into his darkened gaze.

In one fluid movement, he lifted Laura, and as she wrapped her legs around him, he bee-lined for the balcony. Laura's eyes widened when she realized his intention. She wiggled in his arms. "What are you doing?"

"Isn't it obvious?"

"Rob, it's morning. There are people—"

"Relax," he cut in, bracing her on the patio table. "This is our blind spot. No one will see us from here."

"Are you sure?" She was already spreading her legs, her inhibitions flying out the window.

"Positive." He thrust inside her with a groan, filling her, the squelching sound of her wet flesh echoing in the air.

What did it matter if someone saw them, anyway? The thought of being watched was such a turn-on, she half-wished Rob's words weren't true. Her eyelids flickered shut as he fucked her with slow, steady thrusts, getting deeper each time. The hardness of the table pressed into her skin, giving her a slight discomfort, but she didn't care. She needed this. She needed him.

Her eyes flew open, meeting his intense stare that triggered an instant stomach flip. *This is crazy, nothing but good sex. There's no way I'm falling for this man.*

Pushing the insane feelings aside, she tightened her legs around his waist, her body welcoming his rough strokes. Head-to-toe pleasure overwhelmed her. The urge to moan his name was almost too much to bear. She gave in to it, uncaring that it would blow their cover. The anticipated climax hit her like a blast, stealing every ounce of her energy. This time Rob didn't come with her; she thought he'd stopped when he pulled out, but he only led her to the edge of the balcony and made her to grip onto the balustrade. Her face was in the wind, her back turned to him as she overlooked the sea in front of her.

Just as she turned her head to look over her shoulders, Rob placed a hand on her shoulder and rammed into her. Laura's knees buckled, a loud scream escaping her lips as the rough penetration assaulted her still-sensitive flesh. She gripped the wall tighter, managing to push out her ass some more while her tits jiggled in her chest. Rob slammed into her several times, his moans deep as her pussy clenched him over and over again.

"I think I'm gonna come again!" Laura exclaimed between moans.

"Then come, Sweetheart," he said, voice rough and husky as he continued to plunge into her. Laura squealed, her flesh clinging onto him tightly as her body convulsed once again. Her knees weakened and she felt as if she was going to fall on her face but with Rob's hand on her shoulder, it gave her some steadiness. She could feel her juices seep from around his cock and trail down her legs, making the contact of skin-to-skin sound even sloppier. He glided inside her fluidly, hitting that spot she loved so much while her body trembled. Laura was at a loss for words and felt like she would lose her mind at any moment now.

Rob's hand tightened on her shoulder and she braced herself as his manhood twitched inside her. He bucked inside her a couple times, pausing when just the tip was inside of her and then he spurted his cum inside her. Laura continued to quiver as the warmth spilled into and out of her, fogging the floor and trailing down her legs. When Rob pulled out, her knees buckled, but he swept her into his arms and carried her to the bed.

Rob placed her limp body on the bed, but he didn't join her. Still panting, she turned on her side, watching as he reached for his shirt.

"Leaving?" she asked, a sudden pang in her stomach.

He turned and glanced at her, then pulled the shirt over his head. "Yeah, I have a few things to take care of."

"Will I see you again?" The words left her mouth before she could stop them. She pushed up to sit, wrapping the sheet around her. "I mean, if you want to, that is."

Rob glanced down then back at her, the reluctance obvious on his face. "I would like to, Laura, but—"

"It's fine." Her face burned with embarrassment. *Why did I open my big mouth? This was a one-night stand that went in overtime. We should have parted ways hours ago.*

"Let me finish," he said, moving closer to the bed. "I'd love to, but I already have plans. Unless, you want to come with me."

"I'd like that," Laura replied with a grin.

Chapter 4

Rob gave the server a smile as she placed the cup of coffee on the table. She smiled in return, her appreciative eyes roaming over him. He had long gotten used to the lingering stares from women; hell, he often capitalized on it. The notches on his bedpost were too many to count. His eyes briefly lingered on her ass as she walked away, then he reached for his coffee, taking a sip. If there was one thing Italians knew best, it was how to brew their coffee. The café near Laura's hotel served the best he'd ever tasted.

After leaving her room, he'd returned to the apartment he leased for his trip, showered and shaved, then came back to pick her up. He didn't trust himself to be alone with her again, so he opted to wait for her nearby.

Taking another sip, Rob thought back to last night. He didn't know whether to kick himself for giving in to his urges or surrender to the bliss the memories gave him. Mostly, he didn't regret it. He enjoyed being with her. He'd never met a woman like her, never been affected by a woman like this. Not since—

He shook his head to clear the irritating thoughts of his ex. No. He refused to let her live rent free in his head. She had moved on, and so did he. There was no love lost between them, just anger. Her actions scarred him, ruined him for other women. Because of her, he would never love again.

This was a mistake. Inviting Laura was the rashest decision he'd ever made. No, scratch that. Going up to her hotel room last night was his biggest blunder. He should have taken his helmet, bid her goodnight and went on his way. Instead, he allowed his carnal urges to take over. The consequences would be brutal. They always were. He braced himself for them. Plus, this was a woman mourning a breakup – using him to numb the pain of her failed relationship. He was a rebound, plain and simple and that slightly stung, Rob began to realize. As great as the sex was, the idea of a relationship between them was nearly impossible seeing the shaky foundation it started on. A woman who was not over her ex was bound to crawl back to him if the opportunity presented itself. It was better for everybody if this was nothing more than a brief fling.

But it was so hard rejecting Laura when she lashed him with those big, beautiful eyes that tugged at his heartstrings. How could he say no?

With Laura, there was a familiar, pulse-tripping sensation that made him wary. This was a woman he'd just met; why was he reacting to her like this?

Rob took another sip of the coffee, suddenly wishing it was a glass of scotch. Never mind his feelings, his conscience was telling him something else. *The* age gap. Laura was obviously young for someone like him. Almost half his age.

She is young, but she isn't a child. She's quite capable of making her own decisions.

Regardless, he needed to take a hands-off approach. No touching. Definitely no kissing or fucking. This was a casual day out. A friendly date, of sorts. He would never see her again after today.

He drank the remaining coffee as Laura entered the cafe wearing another bright sundress and a smile, his jacket over her shoulders. He gave her a peck on the cheek and signaled to the server to order breakfast. As Laura tried to order in an amusing broken Italian, he noticed something different about her. She seemed brighter and more confident. Very sexy. He liked it.

"So what were your plans for today?" he asked as she sipped her latte.

"No plans," she said. "I threw out my itinerary yesterday. It reminded me of the plans my ex made for the trip, so—" She shrugged, a dark expression forming. With a sweep of her hand, she brushed it away. "I wanted to visit an art gallery yesterday, but it was closed. Antonio Ricci is one of my favorite artists, so it's been a real bummer—"

"I know Antonio. He's a friend of mine."

Laura gaped. "You're kidding, right?"

He shook his head. "Antonio and I go way back. I've purchased several of his paintings whenever I'm in town. He closes his shop whenever he gets a burst of inspiration to paint. He has to, or else the idea will escape. Do you want to go see him?"

"I would love you!"

Rob's brows lifted. Laura instantly turned bright red, waving her hands around. "No, I didn't mean that. I meant to say, I would love to. I'm so sorry!"

"Do you always say you're sorry when you say you love someone?" he teased.

"No, I don't." she sighed, palming her face. "Oh, my God. I can't believe I just said that."

"Relax. It's just a slip of the tongue, isn't it?"

Her head shot up. "Of course," she hurriedly replied.

"I'll call him up to see if we can drop by his studio this afternoon."

"God, I could kiss you right now." She reddened, palming her face again. "Me and my big mouth."

Rob groaned inside, realizing this would be a long, tortuous day.

AFTER ROB TOOK CARE of business, they spent the morning touring museums and popping into little antique shops. Laura bought a disposable camera, and although he hated taking photos, Rob eventually gave in and posed for a photo. Just before the camera flashed, he gave her a kiss on the cheek. She looked very pleased, and it made him happy.

By lunchtime, Rob took her to a restaurant overlooking the city. He'd been there several times before, usually by himself, so he could reserve his favorite spot, tucked away in a little corner of the dining area. Laura kept snapping photos until the food arrived. She happily feasted on her pasta, and he opted for his favorite cut of steak. They shared a bottle of wine, and he insisted on paying the bill. After lunch, they took a quick walk in a nearby park and stopped by the Trevi fountain again.

"This feels like we've come full circle, doesn't it?" Laura asked, staring at the fountain. Rob caught the quick gaze she sent his way and the soft blush on her cheeks.

"You're right, I guess. Is it me, or does it feel longer than a day?"

"It feels like forever," she replied, turning to him. "Do you believe in fate, Rob?"

"Do you?" he countered, deliberately sidestepping the question.

She shrugged. "I can't help wondering if you and I were meant to meet. The way it unfolded was too co-incidental, don't you think?"

"And if we were, what do you think that means?"

Again, that blush. "I've never slept with a guy on the first... whatever this was, but I enjoyed it."

"I did, too, Laura."

She moved closer. "I was thinking... if you're not busy, and I'm not busy, we could hang out again. I'm leaving tomorrow, so..."

He squeezed her hand. "Something to think about, Laura. Come on. Let's get going. Antonio's expecting us."

After one last stop at a café for Frappuccino, they headed to Antonio's studio. Rob led her through the back gate that opened to a beautiful walled garden. The artist soon appeared through a door, wearing a long tunic over satin pants and leather shoes.

"Robert!" his heavy, sultry accent washed over them.

Rob returned his hug and kissed him on both cheeks. "Antonio. It's been a while. I'm glad to see you."

"Here to buy another one from my collection?" Antonio asked with grin. "I can always count on your patronage whenever you stop by."

"As if you need it. I heard the buzz about your plans to launch a gallery in New York. I can imagine how busy you must be."

"Not too busy for the man who made this possible."

Rob shook his head. "All I did was put a few feelers out. Your talent did most of the work."

"Either way, I'm forever in your debt."

Again, Rob dismissed his comment. "Actually, I'm here for a private tour," he replied, taking Laura's hand. "And I brought a friend."

Antonio gave them a playful smirk, his thick eyebrows lifting. "Oh, he's never brought a friend before," he said, reaching to kiss Laura's hand. "Welcome darling. Call me Antonio."

Laura's smile spread from ear to ear. "It's such an honor to meet you, Antonio. I'm a great fan of your work."

"Laura is an artist, too," Rob offered, and Laura's eyes flew around to meet his, her expression aghast.

"Barely. My sketches are nowhere as stunning as your art, Antonio," she said.

"She's selling herself short, I promise."

"I take your word as law, Rob. Laura, I'd love to see your work someday."

A thunderstruck Laura gripped his hand as Antonio let them into his studio and ushered them into a grand receiving area. "Give me a moment," he said while wandering into another room.

"Oh, my God, did you hear what he said?" Laura whispered. "He wants to see my work!"

"He sure does," Rob replied, smiling affectionately. She was so cute when flustered, her blush covering her neck.

"That's crazy, though! I'm not ready."

"I'm sure he'll still be interested when you're ready, Laura. Take all the time you need."

"I'm so nervous, I need to pee. Where's the ladies' room?"

Rob gestured down the hall with a jerk of his head. "It's the last door on your right." He watched as she walked away. Yes, he was certainly in trouble.

Antonio's throat-clearing made him turn around. The older man's amused stare made him scoff. "What?"

"She's not just a friend, is she?" Antonio asked.

Rob nodded. "She's just someone I met yesterday, that's it."

"Really? The way she stared at you, one would assume it's been longer than a day."

"You've always had an overactive imagination, Antonio."

"And you have never been friendly with a woman you haven't taken to bed."

"My sex life is none of your business."

The other man smiled briefly. "Touché. Still, it would be careless of me not to point out how smitten she is with you."

Rob glanced down the hallway, then back at Antonio. "Didn't I just mention your overactive imagination? Laura and I just met. There's no way she has feelings for me."

A memory surfaced of their conversation at the Trevi fountain. Was Antonio right? He breathed a sigh, catching his friend's knowing stare.

"You're not blind, Robert, neither are you stupid. You've broken many hearts before, but never a child's."

"She's not a child," he gritted. "She's twenty-three years old."

"Let me correct myself. She's younger than your usual."

Rob said nothing.

"Don't you think it's time to settle down again? I understand it's difficult after what—"

Rob quickly waved him into silence as Laura reappeared, smiling. "Much better. I'm ready for that tour."

"You must forgive me, darlings. I'm too busy to take you on the tour myself. I've struck inspiration, you see, and I must paint them before they flitter away. Robert dear, if you fancy something, feel free to take it and just send me the check," Antonio said, leading the way to a private part of his studio where a large canvas stood against the wall with splatters of paint.

"Another one of my works in progress," Antonio said. He then dismissed them with a playful wave of his hand. "Off you go then. I must get on with my work. Tell Denise to close the studio when you go out, darlings. Have fun!" With a wink, he disappeared into his painting room.

"How long have you known Antonio?" Laura asked as they walked into the empty yet well-lit gallery room.

"Quite a while," Rob replied. "I bought his paintings when he was an emerging artist selling his work in the streets. We quickly became friends afterwards."

"It must be cool to be friends with a world-renowned artist."

"Our friendship has its perks, like now," he said. "The gallery is closed to the public, yet we have access."

They walked in silence for the next several minutes, admiring each painting displayed on the wall. Laura tucked away her camera and decided to take in the experience. When they reached the end of the exhibit, she turned around to face him. "Thank you so much for bringing me here. It means a lot to me."

"You're welcome. I'm glad you like it."

She moved closer, her fingers gently stroking his chest. The tingle in Rob's spine confirmed how deeply fucked he was. The more his conscience warned him to leave her alone, the more he wanted her. His impulses were out of control. There was no way to reel them back in.

Rob cupped her cheeks and gently pulled her in. The paintings on the wall were the only witnesses to their kiss. When they finally broke apart, Rob realized that this time, it would be harder to walk away.

THE BUZZING OF LAURA'S cell phone woke her from a deep slumber. It was the last day of her trip to Rome, and she intended to sleep in late. She pushed to sit, annoyed at having to leave Rob's warmth. *Whoever it is, their reason for calling better be good.*

It was Belinda. She checked the time. It was almost six in the morning. Not wanting to wake Rob up, Laura lifted the phone, slipped into a robe, and took the call on the balcony. She swiped the screen, placing the phone to her ear.

"Oh, my God, Laura! I've been calling you for ages!" Belinda exclaimed the second the line opened. "Why haven't you called me back?"

"I've been busy. You told me to have fun, remember?"

"I know, but it's not like you not to call me back. I've been wondering if you've already met Adam's replacement."

Laura glanced at Rob's sleeping form. Her face warmed at the memory of his tongue on her body last night. He'd dropped her off after they left the studio, and she convinced him to come up for a nightcap. Their clothes were on the floor within a few minutes of entering the apartment.

Belinda gasped. "You've met someone, haven't you?"

"No, I haven't," Laura, replied, again looking over at the sleeping figure on her bed. She wanted Rob to be her secret.

"You liar!" Belinda squealed. "You have to tell me about it. I should have known from the moment you didn't call me back. Ah! This is great, Laura!"

Laura laughed. "Belinda, I'm telling you, it's nothing."

"Yeah, right. You sound like a woman who got the best sex of her life. Come on, tell me all about this new boy toy of yours."

"He's not a boy toy," Laura replied, closing her eyes at the slip of her tongue.

Her best friend giggled. "Oh, so there *is* a he."

Laura sighed. "It's nothing, really. It's not like I'm dating him."

"It's still an amazing thing, Laura. The sooner you forget whatever-his-name-is, the better. I'm happy for you. I really am."

"Thank you." Laura couldn't stop the smile from pulling her lips apart. Belinda was right. Being with Rob had tempered the heartbreak. She thought of Adam, and there was no sorrow in her heart. She wasn't over him, not by a long shot, but she could return to New York with a smile.

A sudden shuffle had Laura looking towards the bedroom where she saw Rob getting out of bed with nothing on. Her body instantly grew heated as she watched, feeling compelled to just blatantly stare.

"Laura? Did you hear what I said?" Belinda asked.

"Laura!"

"What?"

"Oh, my God. Are you with him?" Belinda asked with an excited gasp.

"I'll see you tomorrow, Belinda," she whispered hurriedly in the phone, peeling it from her ears.

"Oh, come on. Don't leave me hanging."

"Bye!"

Laura hung up and returned to the room. Last night was amazing, even better than before. It wasn't just about the sex; it was the way he held her afterwards, the safety in his arms. His tender kisses on her shoulder, the affection in his eyes made her wish this was more than a two-day fling. It was crazy, but she couldn't help the way he made her feel.

Rob returned from the bathroom, interrupting her thoughts, greeting her with a kiss on her cheeks. She gasped as he suddenly lifted her, and they tumbled back into bed.

"So, what do you want to do on your last day in Rome?"

"I'd like to have dinner later..."

"And?"

Laura pushed up on her knees, gently pinned him down on the bed with her weight. "Maybe spend the rest of the day here?" she smirked.

"I like where this is going." He raised his head and kissed her.

Laura melted from his warm lips. She didn't want to leave this bed again. Hell, the thought of leaving Rome made her stomach sink. She wasn't ready to return to reality, to the environment she struggled to fit in. But this dream had to end. In a few hours, she had to say goodbye and return to New York.

"I don't want to leave," she whispered against his mouth.

Rob grunted in response, deepening the kiss.

She traced her fingers down his back, wanting to remember the touch of his skin, the warmth of his body, the rock-hard feel of him against her. She kissed him back, communicating how much she would miss him. The last two days in Rome had been the best of her life. It was an experience she would never forget.

Rob broke the kiss, his serious eyes searching her face. "What's wrong?"

She shook her head. "Nothing, it's just... I wish I didn't have to leave." The reality of returning to New York with no boyfriend was a reality she didn't want to face.

Rob didn't answer, instead, he took her hand into his and placed it on his chest.

"These last two days were like a dream, and I don't want to wake up."

"You'll have to, eventually," he said with a hint of sadness in his tone.

"I know. I meant... I just—"

He placed his finger on her lips. "We have a few more hours, Laura. How about one more for the road?"

She smiled against his lips and they shared a kiss, Rob rolling to lay on his back while Laura straddled him, staring down at his beautiful face. Her heart skipped a beat in her chest; she slowly peeled off her robe and discarded it to one side, leaving her naked against Rob who was also naked.

He dragged his fingers along her sides and down her thighs, rubbing his hands back and forth against her smooth skin and admiring the plump flesh between. Laura took his length in her hand and ran her hands along it, smearing the pinkish head with the pre-cum that oozed from the tip.

Rob moaned and adjusted himself, propping a pillow underneath his head so he had a better view of what she was doing. Laura eased up, his cock in hand and settled above it, holding it in place before she slowly lowered herself on it. She gasped when the tip was in, her mouth spreading apart as the rigid feel of Rob's manhood familiarized itself with her.

Her eyes fluttered close as she went down a bit more, inch after inch escaping inside. She bit her lips and held onto his hand, a tremor passing through her body when he was buried to the hilt. She opened her eyes to look at him again, realizing that he had that look in his eyes which spoke clearly of his lust. His ears were red and so was his chest, his muscles on full display as she sheathed him with the warmth of her pussy.

Rob gritted his teeth as he watched her, her hair spilling over her shoulders, her eyes sultry as they fluttered open and shut. Her nipples were hard against her chest, her breasts full and firm. His gaze traveled downwards to her flat stomach that sucked in and out from her deep breaths. When he finally arrived at her cavern, he swallowed hard, a bolt of pleasure rushing through him as he filled his vision with the sight of her spread lips and the juices that glistened there. He was completely buried inside her and he felt proud of her for taking his cock more easily each day. Her clit rested on his groin area. He was tempted to touch her but he wanted to watch her get off on his cock even more.

Laura started to rotate her hips, feeling a liquid rush inside her as her arousal heightened. It always amazed her how good Rob felt inside her, how well he fitted and how her entire body was able to respond from a single thrust. She closed her eyes and arched her back, resting her hands against his legs. She rotated her hips and bounced a little, all of it feeling too good to be true. When the pleasure grew more intense and Laura could feel the weight of her orgasm getting closer, she began to move even faster, gasping between moans as she abandoned herself to the pleasure she was feeling.

She felt Rob's hands at her hips again and her eyes opened up to the image of him, their gazes locking. Laura eased up a little, Rob lifting her a bit before he pulled her down on his length.

"Fuck!" Laura gasped from the sharp thrusts, his cock slamming inside her.

Rob directed her movements, leading her back and forth on his length and enjoying the slapping sounds it made. She was perfect, and incredibly snug around him that he thought he'd bust soon, but he tried to hold out as best as he could.

"Mmm, this feels so freaking good!" she exclaimed, her body flushed from his ministrations.

Rob eased up from the pillow and wrapped his hands around her, his face coming up right between her breasts. He caught a nipple in his mouth and sucked hard, enjoying the way her pussy tightened immediately at the act. He pulled her down on him and Laura whimpered, feeling herself coming close to the end.

Rob did too, but today was the last day they would see each other again and he wanted to make the most of it. In one slight movement, he flipped her on her back and joined their bodies again in a single thrust. Laura screamed, her legs closing in a little, but Rob quickly pried them apart, propping one leg against his chest as he fucked her deep and hard.

He felt his orgasm coming on and as much as he wanted to hold out, Laura's pussy was just too good for him to slow down. He continued to drill her, the slaps echoing in the room along with her moans. His cock swelled inside her and with one final push, he came, grunting. Laura shivered, the feeling of his cum inside her triggering her own orgasm. Her walls tightened around him and she tightly closed her eyes, trying to calm her galloping heart.

Rob held his cock and pulled it from inside her, realizing he was still hard this time around. His manhood glistened with their juices and he muttered a curse, watching as Laura's small hole closed up when he pulled himself from her. His cream flowed from her depths and slithered to her ass in the most beautiful way.

Gritting his teeth, Rob held his member and scooped it up, directing it inside her once again. His overly sensitive cock massaged her creamy walls yet again and he shuddered from the oversensitivity.

"Oh, Rob." Her voice was sultry and sweet, lacking strength but still managing to arouse every inch of him.

He moved on top of her, their slippery body gliding against each other fluidly with the sweat from their lovemaking. Rob suckled on her slightly salty neck and dragged his tongue all the way to her mouth; all the while with his cock still inside her. Laura moaned against his lips, barely finding the energy, but oh it felt good to have him sliding inside her extremely wet flesh. The heat from their bodies made it even more overwhelming for her but she basked in every moment.

He moved inside her until she could feel him hardening even more, his movements faster, but still gentle. She wrapped her legs around him, wanting to be closer to him than she already was. Her fingers trailed down his back, her nails digging into his skin. The room wreaked of soap and sex, but Laura loved everything about it. She closed her eyes again and moaned as Rob's hands slid over her breast, his mouth on hers while his cock gently stirred her insides.

The distribution drove her insane and almost brought her to the point of tears. In a few hours she would have to say goodbye to all of this and she was by no means ready; still, she knew it had to be done.

Rob bucked inside her, his cock driving even further. Laura gasped and dug her nails into his back, unintentionally breaking his flesh when her orgasm took her by surprise. Her body thrashed on the bed, her moans unending as she hugged his stellar manhood. With a grunt, she knew Rob came too. That and the warm sensation flooding inside her.

His weight rested on her as they came and although he was heavy, Laura didn't mind. She reveled in every moment, her lips tipping into a smile when his cock slipped from inside her. Rob rolled to the side, breathing heavily. Laura rushed to snuggle up beside him, not wanting the moment to end, but knowing that very soon it would.

Her heart felt torn by that one simple fact.

Chapter 5

Laura sighed as the city of Rome grew smaller from her window. The plane had taken off several minutes ago and yet, she already missed the city's European charm and the man whose arms she'd left several hours ago.

She rested her head against the seat, blowing another breath as the memories of Rob's touch filled her. They'd stayed in bed the entire morning, making love like it was their last day on earth. In a way, it seemed like it was.

God, she already missed him, how sexy he made her feel between the sheets. She missed being in his strong arms, wished she could trace the tattoo on his back again. She wanted to feel the rhythm of his heart against her hand one more time.

They talked a lot. He mostly did the talking, though. She didn't think her university stories would interest a man of the world. He told her more stories of places he'd visited and the people he'd met, but Laura never asked about his personal life. She knew he was divorced and had one child, but it wasn't her place to ask for details he hadn't offered. It was just as well, anyway. It would have been harder to say goodbye.

By lunchtime, they ordered takeout, what Rob considered Rome's best pizza. He was right, though. It was another thing she would miss about the city; how great their food was.

Rob was probably the most intense man she'd ever met, but he had a great sense of humor, too. She remembered laughing at a particular joke he made as they sat half-naked eating pizza and drinking coffee from paper cups, and she accidentally spilled coffee on her chest. She went straight to the bathroom to clean up, and Rob followed. What transpired next made her cheeks heat as she recalled the memory of his tongue between her thighs. She would never look at a bathroom sink the same way again.

It was late afternoon when they left the hotel room, and he took her to a vintage theater to watch a French film he had already seen several times. Laura had no clue what the movie was about. She was too caught up with the sweet taste of his lips. After the film, and with arms linked, he took her to his favorite restaurant. It was smaller and more intimate than the ones they'd been before. He knew the chef by name, and they were seated at the farthest booth for privacy, which gave him the opportunity to run his hand up her leg whenever he wanted. She left the restaurant so hot and bothered, so ready for him to take her. It could be anywhere. She didn't care.

They made love until one in the morning, when an alarm reminded Laura of her flight in three hours. Rob sat in the armchair, silently watching as she packed her luggage. She had nothing to say, either. She knew, sensing the heavy atmosphere, that he was finding it hard to say goodbye, too.

A slight tension settled between them as Rob accompanied her to the airport. They made one last stop at an indoor cafe for coffee. He mentioned returning to New York later in the day, and although she wanted to ask for his number, she didn't. It would mean breaking the rule. They had decided this was a onetime thing, so reuniting in New York would mean breaking that agreement. Plus, she didn't want to seem desperate, not even a little. She had just got out of a serious relationship, and she didn't want to start another one right off the bat.

They walked until they reached her gate. Here, it was time to say goodbye. Rob took her hands, giving them a squeeze, triggering an ache in her stomach. The intercom announcer interrupted the stare between them. Time to go. Time to move on from this fantasy.

"Well..." Laura took a deep breath. "I guess this is it." *I wish you would ask me to stay.*

Rob smiled. "Yes, this is it."

"Thanks for saving my life," she replied, summoning a smile. "And for taking me around Rome."

"It was my pleasure." He leaned forward and gave her a quick hug.

"Goodbye," she whispered, the emotion rising her chest. She blinked, surprised by the tears in her eyes.

"Take care of yourself, Laura."

She felt his burning stare as she walked away, but she didn't look back. She couldn't.

IT WAS HALF-PAST FIVE when Laura arrived home, exhausted and grumpy. The out-of-service elevator did not improve her mood. She wasn't looking forward to dragging her luggage up the three flights to her apartment. The journey took forever, and she let out an exasperated sigh when she reached her floor. She was almost at her door when Mrs. Kadinsky, her elderly neighbor exited her apartment with a smile. Laura groaned inside. She adored Mrs. Kadinsky, but the older woman could talk for hours without stopping. Usually, she didn't mind, but she was half-dead on her feet with the only intention to collapse in bed.

"Oh, you're back dear!" Mrs. Kadinsky said. "I'm so glad. I missed our little talks. It's been so lonely since you left. My son barely calls anymore, not to mention the grandkids. You'd think I have no family the way they keep ignoring me."

Oh, boy. "Hi, Mrs. K, it's good to be back."

"How was your trip?" she asked. "Oh, Rome is such a nice place this time of year, isn't it?"

Laura nodded, still panting, the sweat running down her face. Mrs. Kadinsky didn't seem to notice. The elderly woman launched into an anecdote of her time in Rome during the sixties.

"Mrs. K," Laura said, interrupting the story. "I don't mean to be rude, but I need to get some rest."

"No worries. We can catch up later, right?"

"Sorry, Mrs. K. No can do. I'm meeting Belinda for drinks tonight. She's getting married in two months."

"Belinda? That cute little blonde who always drops by? Oh, what a wonderful thing." She smiled dreamily. "I do love weddings!"

"Mrs. K, is there anything you need? I really need to go."

"Okay, dear, we'll catch up later, won't we?"

"Sure thing!" Laura replied, slipping the key into the lock, intending to slip into a much-needed sleep coma.

THERE'S SOMETHING DIFFERENT about you," Belinda commented as Laura slipped onto the stool beside her. "You seem... I don't know, more alive, maybe?"

Laura shrugged, glancing at the mirror behind the bar. She'd given her hair a quick wash before leaving the apartment and applied light makeup on her face, but that was about it. Nothing special. "I have no idea."

"There's this glow on your face I've never seen before. You look like a woman who's had the time of her life."

Laura waved to the bartender, scoffing. "You're fishing." She'd only known Belinda for two years, but it was long enough to identify when she was up to no good.

"So what if I am?" Belinda slumped on her stool with a pout. "Your lips have been locked tighter than a vault since you got back."

"I've only been home for half a day, Belinda."

"That's long enough. Come on, spill. What happened in Rome?"

The bartender interrupted their conversation, and Laura ordered her favorite cocktail before turning to her best friend once more. "Sex happened, Belinda. Sex with a really hot guy."

"Oooh. Tell me more. Was he any good?"

A slow smile spread across Laura's face, and she nodded slowly.

"Oh, come on, don't be a prude." Belinda pouted. "Tell me! I swear if you're leaving out anything, I will disown you!"

Laura palmed her cheeks with a grin. "It was so good. Amazing. I'm dickmatized, seriously. The way he made me feel was so out of this world. I can't explain. I can't stop thinking about the things he did with his—"

"Okay, stop. I changed my mind. I'm already jealous. How about you tell me what you did out of bed?"

Laura smirked, launching into details of her trip.

"He sounds like a special guy, Laura," Belinda said, taking a sip of her drink. "Do you plan on seeing him again?"

"No. We agreed it was a fling, nothing else."

"Oh, scandalous." Belinda gave an exaggerated gasp. "Did you at least get his number?"

"No."

"What? Why didn't you?"

Laura sighed. "I told you; we agreed it was just a fling. Having his phone number would defeat the purpose, wouldn't it?"

"Not if you want another taste..."

"I don't."

"Liar."

Laura huffed. "Okay fine, I lied. I would give anything to be with him again."

"Saucy. I've got to say Laura, your trip to Rome really changed you," Belinda said.

"What do you mean?"

"Don't take it the wrong way, but this, it's *so* unlike you to engage in an affair with a stranger."

"What? I can be spontaneous and daring!"

"Ha!" Belinda reached for her drink. "This coming from the woman who orders the same thing every time we eat out."

"Whatever."

"Except... it seems like you've fallen for him."

Laura chuckled. "What? That's ridiculous."

"Is it?" Belinda asked, eyeing her closely. "I've never seen you gush over a guy like this, not even Adam. Speaking of which, is it safe to assume you're already over him?"

"We were together for two years. Of course, I'm not over him, but I don't want him back, that's for sure. What I want is a decent explanation. He owes me that, at least."

"Mmh." Belinda fiddled with her straw; her eyes locked to the bar counter. "I'm sorry that happened to you, Laura. Truly."

"Thanks. I'll be okay."

"Good." Belinda's face brightened. "Now, let's get back to your Roman dreamboat."

"He's not my anything," Laura replied, blushing. "He's someone's ex-husband, someone's dad."

"Wait a minute. How old is he?"

Laura palmed her face, peering at Belinda through her fingers. "Forty-four."

"Forty—" Belinda gasped. "Laura, he's old enough to be your dad! Hell, he's the same age as *my* dad. That's so gross. Oh, my God."

"Can you lower your voice?" Laura hissed, glancing around the bar, but there was no one looking their way. "So what if he's an older guy? He's not my dad. Or yours. In fact, he looks nowhere near forty."

Belinda shrugged. "Whatever works for you, I guess. It's not like you'll see him again, anyway."

"Right." Laura forced a smile, though the thought alone saddened her.

Why can't I forget about him?

"Anyway, end of discussion. Let me see that gorgeous ring."

Belinda squealed in excitement.

Chapter 6

"For the last time, Mom, don't worry about not making it. It's just a graduation ceremony, not my wedding."

"I know, honey, but I'm still bummed. Stupid me for falling and injuring my ankle at a time like this."

Laura rested the phone against her ear and reached into her school bag for her keys. "The most important thing is that you're fine. It could have been worse. I don't know why you keep taking risks like that."

"Oh, stop being dramatic. It was just a simple hike. I've been a little careless, that's all."

"I wish you would stop. It's not healthy for me to worry about you like this."

"And I wish you would loosen up. Live a little. Stop worrying about me."

"I can't."

"When was the last time you tried being spontaneous? You wouldn't be so intense if you let go for once."

Laura dropped her bag on the couch, her thoughts drifting to Rome, Rob and their two-day steam fest. She'd never released her inhibitions like that, and she never would again. "I'm not intense, Mom, I'm just careful."

"Mmh. How has careful been treating you so far? You're leaving college soon. It's time to live your best life."

"You're a bad influence, you know that?"

"And you're just like your dad, God rest his soul. He toed the line his entire life. I don't want that for you, honey. I want you to enjoy life."

"I am enjoying life."

"Have you been on a date since you and Adam broke up?"

"Gosh, Mom, it's only been two weeks." She loosened the scrunchie and set her tresses free. Her shoes followed suit.

"Remember my motto?"

Laura rolled her eyes. "It's a stupid motto. I can't use another guy as a rebound. I need to get over Adam on my own."

Isn't that what I tried to do with Rob, though? Didn't I use him to cure my heartbreak?

She didn't count on it backfiring, though. Their time together shouldn't have stained her soul like this. It should have been a fling, nothing else. Now, two weeks later, she still struggled to forget him.

Her doorbell rang as she attempted to unbutton her jeans. She peeked through the peephole, sighing at Mrs. Kadinsky's smiling face. Knowing her neighbor, she would keep knocking until Laura answered the door.

"Mom, I have to go. Talk to you later, okay? And please, get some rest. Stay off your injured foot."

"I won't make any promises."

"Mom!"

"Just kidding, honey," her mom replied, chuckling. Laura groaned in frustration as she ended the call. Forcing a smile, she opened the door.

"Mrs. K, what's up?"

The older woman's smile deflated as if she realized Laura's smile wasn't real. "Is everything okay, Laura?"

"Of course." She reached out, giving Mrs. Kadinsky a reassuring pat on her arm. "Just some terrible news about my mom. She broke her ankle on a hiking trip."

"I'm so sorry."

"It's fine. She's recovering."

Mrs. Kadinsky's face brightened once more. "Well, I have some news to brighten your day. Wait a minute. I'll be back."

She returned to her apartment, and after a loud shuffling, emerged with a large package. "This came for you a few hours ago, dear," she said, handing the package to Laura.

Laura brows lifted, scanning the large package wrapped with tape marked fragile. "Me? Are you sure?" Except her mom, no one had ever sent her a gift before.

"Oh, yes," Mrs. Kadinsky said. "I told Freddie to just leave it with me. The poor man had to drag it all the way up the stairs. He was sweating like a pig when he got here. I gave him a glass of lemonade..."

As Mrs. Kadinsky went on about Freddie the delivery man, Laura reached for the package, feeling around the hard edges. It was a painting, that much was sure. A hopeful thought formed, but she pushed it aside. No way did Rob send her a gift. He had already forgotten their little affair.

"Thank you, Mrs. K." Laura gave her a polite smile. "I need to get ready for Belinda's engagement party."

"Of course, dear! Tell Belinda congratulations for me, will you?"

"Yes, I certainly will."

Laura closed her door, still eyeing the package where she'd rested it on the floor. The urge to open it battled with the fear of being wrong. She didn't want the disappointment if she discovered it wasn't from Rob. Making a mental note to check when she was emotionally stable, she hopped into the shower. It was almost six. The party was at seven. She'd hate to disappoint Belinda by being late. After a quick shower, she slipped into her favorite black dress and pulled on a pair of stilettos that made her long legs even sexier. The golden hour sunshine seeped through her windows and flooded her studio apartment. She checked the time; fifteen minutes to spare.

She glanced at the package again. *Just open it, Laura, it's the only way you'll know who sent it.*

Blowing a nervous breath, she took a pair of scissors from her desk and unwrapped the mysterious package, gasping when it was revealed.

She carefully pulled out a framed abstract painting created by Antonio. She remembered admiring this piece at the gallery. It was a purple and pink artwork titled 'Lovers.' With shaking hands, she settled it on the floor. Before she turned away, she noticed a small note sticking to the back. It was a piece of stationery from the hotel, the messy handwriting scripting the words, "I'll see you in my dreams, -R."

A surge of bittersweet emotions took over. She leaned against the wall, giggling with tear-filled eyes.

He remembers me.

He's been thinking of me.

Why did he send this painting, though? Does this mean he wants more? Do I hope?

How did he find me, anyway?

A sudden knock on the door forced her to compose herself. She dabbed her eyes before opening the door to Belinda's wide grin. "Surprise!"

Laura blinked, taking her best friend's head-to-toe perfection, her diamond-studded dress clinging to her curves. Her golden hair was like a waterfall cascading over her shoulders.

"What are you doing here?"

"I'm here for you, duh," Belinda says. "Ronaldo's downstairs with the limo, but don't worry, take your time. I'm the bride. They can all wait for me."

"What about Henry? I thought you would be going together."

Belinda flashed her a smile while breezing into the apartment. "Henry can wait, too."

Laura caught a hint of anger in her tone, but it contradicted the sparkle in her eyes. "Is everything okay, Belinda?"

"Of course. It's fabulous. Henry and I have never been better." She smiled again, eyeing Laura's outfit. "I suspected you would wear a black dress. Black is definitely not back, darling."

"You're changing the subject."

"And you're wearing an abomination. What happened to that gorgeous gown I bought for your birthday? It fit you so well."

Laura's mind flashed to the thousand-dollar satin gown hanging in her closet, the stark reminder of how contrasting their lives were. She would never feel comfortable dressed in an outfit that cost more than her month's rent. "I'll wear it some other time. I don't want to upstage the bride, after all," she said with a grin.

"As if." Belinda scoffed, twirling. "Have you seen me?" Her giggle paused as her gaze landed on the painting. "Oh, what is *this*?"

Laura groaned inwardly as Belinda walked over to the painting, her curious eyes catching the note. *Damn it. I should have put that away.* "Uh -"

"Oh, my God!" Belinda shrieked as she read the note. "I'll see you in my dreams! R! Is this from him?"

Laura snatched the note from her hand and tucked it in her top drawer. "It's nothing."

"What do you mean it's nothing? That has got to be the sweetest note I've ever read!"

"You think so?" Laura asked.

"Well, it is a bit corny," Belinda replied with a giggle. "Come on! You have to tell me more about this guy! Where is he from? Is he Italian? Because you know they say European men have really -"

"No, he's from New York," Laura interrupted. "And I already told you; I don't know much about him."

"Really?" Belinda said, clearly not satisfied. "You're not leaving anything out, are you?"

Laura rolled her eyes, removing her necklace from her drawer. She placed it around her neck and turned her back to Belinda. "Stop fishing and quit trying to distract me from what I asked earlier. Are you and Henry okay?"

Belinda locked the necklace and twisted Laura to face her. "We're fine, Laura. Truly. How are you holding up?" she asked, concern etched on her face. "I know Adam meant a lot to you."

Laura put on a smile. It was easier to forget her breakup in Rome when she was away from everything and everyone she knew. But now she had returned to New York, everything reminded her of her ex. Even though Adam was a jerk at the end, they still had good times too. Now, every street they walked, every restaurant they ate in, and every dark corner they kissed in would be marked forever. There was no escape. "He did, but let's not talk about him. Tonight is about you."

Belinda's concern switched to sympathy. Leaning in, she enveloped Laura in a warm hug. "I'm glad you're okay. Someday, this will be a distant memory, a story you tell your kids."

"I hope."

A sudden knock on the door made them break apart, and Laura moved to answer. The short, middle-aged man gave her a brilliant smile.

"Miss Laura, you look dashing," he said.

"Thanks, Ronaldo. At least someone appreciates my simplicity," she replied, and Belinda scoffed.

"We'll be right down, Ronaldo," Belinda said behind her. "Give us a minute."

"Sure, no problem. Mr. Henry has been trying to reach you."

"Oh, boy. What now?" Belinda whispered, pulling her phone from the purse.

Laura grabbed her keys and locked the door behind them. Belinda's phone began ringing as they descended in the elevator. A soft sigh left her as she pressed the answer button. Laura listened discreetly. Was there trouble in paradise, as she suspected?

I hope not. One of us deserves a happy ending, at least.

The icy wind blasted Laura's face as they stepped out of the apartment. She pulled the coat around her, the action triggering the memory of Rob's jacket around her shoulders. A warm blush crept into her cheeks, but her friend didn't notice. Belinda's rapid conversation with Henry grew more intense when they slipped into the back of the limo. Distress marred her features when she hung up. She sighed, throwing her head against the seat. "I really need your help, Laura."

"Why? Is Henry okay?" Laura asked, concerned.

"It's not about Henry," she replied. "It's this stupid dinner! I haven't told you this, but Henry's parents are going through a terrible divorce and apparently, they don't want to be seated next to each other."

"Well, can't they put their malice on hold for one night?"

"That's what I said! Oh, my God. They're so selfish it's not even funny. But I've got an even bigger problem."

"What is it?"

"My dad's coming to the dinner too."

"Your dad? I thought you weren't in contact with him."

"Yeah, I wasn't. Things were a little strained between us after he and Mom divorced a few years ago. We've been in dialogue for a few months now, so our relationship is on the mend."

"I'm happy for you, especially now that you'd want him to walk you down the aisle. But I don't see the problem."

Belinda sighed. "He's not a fan of my family, and the feeling is mutual. I need you to keep him company, so he doesn't feel left out. I don't want him to feel discouraged and leave."

Laura imagined a heavyset man with a huge belly and receding hair. "Why me? Can't your friend Amy do it?"

"Well, considering you're my maid of honor, I'd expect you to."

"Oh, my god." Laura grinned. "I'm your maid of honor?"

"Of course, you are! Who else would it be?"

"Your cousin Gina, duh. I can't imagine she's pleased with your decision." Gina and Belinda had been joined at the hip since they were kids. There was no doubt in Belinda's mind that Gina didn't take the news well. "She hates my guts, you know."

"She's just awfully possessive, that's all. Her bark is worse than her bite."

Laura begged to differ, but she didn't want to pursue it. Hanging out with a middle-aged man wasn't the most pleasant task for such an honorable post, but for Belinda's sake, she would be the best maid of honor around.

"So you'll do this for me?" Belinda asked, hands clasped. "I swear, it won't be so bad, I could ask someone else but my dad... he's picky with the people in my circle and truth be told, you're the most down to earth around here. He likes people like you."

Laura sighed. "Well, I don't think it'll be so bad."

"It won't, I promise," she squealed, grinning.

Laura smiled. "Okay, sure; I'll do it."

Chapter 7

Stepping into the Plaza Hotel was like entering another world. The Bancrofts weren't shy about splurging, and it showed. The exquisite ballroom was a blend of classic opulence and timeless elegance. From the twinkling chandeliers to the intricate dinner plates, the Bancrofts didn't leave out any detail. A celebrity band, perfect-looking guests in designer wear, expensive champagne flowing. Laura politely declined a glass from a passing waiter. She was too overwhelmed to drink. Her outfit was a standout and not in a good way. She could have easily been mistaken for an usher instead of a guest. She had never felt so out of place in her life.

As Laura watched the scene unfold, it reminded her of the enormous financial gap between her and Adam. In the past, she would have been here on his arm, trying to fit in, but deep down, she knew it was a fruitless effort. Mostly, she would remain silent, hooked to Adam's arm as they rubbed shoulders with people who were out of her league.

She glanced at Belinda talking to a woman wearing a headset. The wedding planner no doubt. The stress on her face was a dead giveaway. Laura imagined her life if Adam hadn't broken up with her. Would she be in Belinda's place a few years from now, worrying about seating charts and dinner menus, clinging to her fiancé's arm and enduring small talk that left her with a headache?

It's probably why Adam broke up with me, isn't it? He knew I didn't belong in his world. Laura sighed, the emotional tug-of-war too much to bear. She didn't know whether to be relieved or sad.

"Hey, honey."

Laura turned towards the deep voice as Henry Van Doren approached. She didn't miss Belinda's gentle scoff or her slight eye-rolling before she forced a smile. Henry pulled Belinda into his arms, giving her a kiss that made Laura blush. Her eyes shifted to the floor as he eased away.

"Hey, Laura. Nice dress. Suits you well."

"Thanks, Henry."

He smiled, his gaze lingering on her cleavage for a beat, then he leaned in and gave her a peck on the cheek. Laura assessed him as he pulled away. From his haircut down to the shoes, Henry looked like a model from Ralph Lauren. The Van Dorens were classic elite and came from a long line of New York families who ruled the real estate business. Combined with the Bancroft wealth, her best friend would be set for life.

"How was Rome?" he asked. "I'm sorry to hear about you and Adam, but from what I've heard, you're going to be okay."

Laura's brows lifted as Belinda shot him a glare. "I'm sorry sweetie, I told him not to say anything."

"It's fine," Laura reassured her. "It's not like I committed a great sin or anything."

"Depends on how you define *sin*," Henry replied with a wicked grin.

"Can we change the topic, please?" Her sex life—or lack thereof—wasn't up for discussion.

"Henry! Oh, Henry, there you are!"

A tall, auburn-haired woman in a forest green dress sauntered over to them with a martini in hand. "I've been looking all over for you. What are you doing about the seating fiasco?"

"Mother, for the last time, it won't kill you to sit by my father for a few hours. Just... suck it up, please."

Mrs. Van Doren's eyes narrowed. "I refuse to sit beside that cheating asshole. Fix it. Now." She took another sip of her martini before she noticed Laura.

"Can you get me another glass, dear?" she asked.

Laura's face turned bright red, but thankfully, Belinda swooped in.

"Uh, Amelia, this is my maid of honor and best friend, Laura Turner," Belinda introduced them. "Laura, this is Henry's mother, Mrs. Amelia Van Doren."

"Ugh, that wretched last name." Mrs. Van Doren reached for a glass of wine from a nearby waiter. "Tonight can't end fast enough!" She rolled her eyes for extra effect as Henry's lips thinned.

"Mother, please," he muttered. "This is not the place for your drama."

"Oh, my bad, darling." She patted him on the cheek. "Now, would you be a dear and fix the issue? I'd rather sit on the floor than next to your *father*." She gave Belinda a kiss on the cheek and sauntered away to a group of ladies.

Belinda sighed and turned to Laura, "I'm sorry about that. She's quite a handful."

Laura shrugged. "I get it. I wouldn't want to be seated next to Adam, either."

"I don't know what to do, though! We've already planned the seating charts weeks ago, and I don't know who to move."

"Well, who am I sitting next to? I don't mind handling either of the Van Dorens for the night."

Instant relief washed over Belinda's face. "Oh, Laura! Thank you so much!" She signaled to a woman carrying a clipboard. "Let me check the seats."

Her face turned white as she frantically flipped through the charts. "This can't be right." She gaped at the woman who handed her the clipboard. "Are you sure this is it?"

"Quite positive, Miss Bancroft," the woman said stiffly.

"What is it?" Laura asked.

Belinda gave her a pained stare. "It seems that you're seated next to Adam."

A ball of steel formed at the pit of Laura's stomach. "What?"

"I'm so sorry, Laura. I've told mother to uninvite him, but she kept him on the list."

As if she were being summoned, Julie Bancroft eased through the crowd, the splitting image of Belinda, exquisite in a gold sequined dress, her platinum blonde hair in a French updo like her daughter's, and a bright red lipstick that emphasized her full lips.

"Belinda, darling. There you are! Have you met the Rothschilds?"

"*Mother*," Belinda said tightly. "Didn't I tell you to uninvite Adam?"

Julie frowned. "Adam? Dear, we cannot *not* invite the Astors! You know they are close family friends."

"Yes, but this is my wedding, and I don't want him here. You're making this an uncomfortable situation for me."

Laura noticed the distress on Belinda's face and stepped in. "It's alright. This is perfect. Just switch Mrs. Van Doren to Adam's place. It'll work out perfectly."

"Are you sure?"

No. I don't want to be anywhere near that asshole. Out loud, she said, "Don't worry about it. Just enjoy your night, okay?"

Julie shook her head. "Honestly, Belinda. I have no idea what you're so worked up about."

As Julie babbled on, Laura called a nearby server and handed Belinda a martini. Her best friend shot her a thankful smile before drinking it in one go. Julie paused, staring at her daughter with disapproval.

"That's so unladylike."

"I don't care, Mother," Belinda replied, handing the cocktail glass to a passing server. "This is my night. I can do whatever I want."

"Not when it makes us look bad," Julie hissed, blocking her attempt to get another drink. "The last thing I need is you drunk and out of control."

Belinda sighed, backing down immediately. Laura resisted the urge to roll her eyes. Why was Belinda so spineless around her mother? Was it only loyalty or something else?

"Seriously, when is your father coming?" Julie asked, glancing at the entrance.

"He said he'll be here," Belinda insisted.

"Don't count on it. You know what he's like. Thinks he's better than mixing with the likes of us. Imagine..."

"He *said* he'll be here. We both know it's the other way around, Mother, so stop pretending."

"We'll see about that." Julie's face brightened as she glanced behind Belinda's shoulder. "Oh, Adam!" She waved, the action causing a drop in Laura's stomach. Belinda's eyes narrowed at Julie, but she deliberately ignored her daughter's glare.

Laura glanced around for a server, regretting not taking that glass of champagne earlier. It was suddenly hard to breathe. She caught his scent behind her, the familiar woodsy scent that resurrected memories of their romance.

I can't do this. I'm not ready.

But it was too late to move. He was already standing before her, his gaze trained on Julie. The dark circles around his eyes didn't affect how gorgeous he was. His dark hair was a little shorter and faded at the sides.

"Ms. Bancroft." Adam leaned in, giving Julie a kiss on both cheeks.

"Adam, handsome as always. How are you?"

"Never been better." He turned to Belinda, repeating the gesture before returning his attention to Julie. Laura swallowed, embarrassed at being ignored by the man who dumped her without warning. *Is it too much for him to acknowledge me?*

"Excuse me," she whispered to Belinda and scurried off to the powder room. There was no one inside, thankfully, so she could fall apart in peace. Closing the door, she clutched her chest as another panic attack took over.

Breathe, Laura. Just breathe.

Her chest rose and fell with deep, even breaths. The tightening slowly loosened. She closed her stinging eyes, willing the tears to keep at bay.

As long as I'm friends with Belinda, I'll never escape his presence. Is having Belinda in my life worth the agony?

She had to think. To consider. But first, the biggest hurdle remained, facing him across the table.

There's absolutely no way I can do that.

Laura bowed her head, gripping the edge of the sink. *I have to be there for Belinda. She needs me. I can do this. He's just Adam. I can't let him see how much the breakup affects me.*

"Laura?" Belinda's voice suddenly came through the door. Laura reached for a napkin to wipe her eyes.

"Yeah, I'm in here." Moving to the door, Laura let her in.

"Are you okay?" Belinda asked, her worried eyes searching Laura's face. "Why'd you run away?"

"I didn't run away. I couldn't bear being around him. How can he act like I don't exist after what he did to me?"

"Oh, Laura..." Belinda pulled her into a hug. "I'm so sorry. This is all my fault. If I had known about the breakup before the invitations went out—"

"No, it's not your fault, okay? He's an asshole, always will be. Besides, you tried to fix it."

"Little good that did," Belinda scoffed. "I can't believe Mom didn't do what I asked."

Laura took her hand. "Listen, I'm okay. I'll survive."

"At least his parents couldn't come. They're in London."

"Oh, thank God. I can't imagine meeting them for the first time after Adam dumped me."

"Thank you for doing this." Belinda smiled sheepishly. "Because I have another huge favor to ask of you."

"What is it?"

"Mrs. Van Doren was supposed to lead the toast before dinner," Belinda said. "But she drank a little too much. Would you mind filling in, please?"

Laura sighed. Even if she didn't want to, she couldn't escape. Being the maid of honor was slowly becoming a burden she didn't want to handle. "Anything for you," she replied with a tight smile. The thought of standing before a crowd was already making her feel lightheaded.

Gasping delightedly, Belinda swept her in a hug. "Thank you so much. I owe you big time!"

"Don't mention it."

"At least let me retouch your makeup. It's a little smeared."

Ditching her sadness, Laura made a conscious effort to stand taller as they exited the powder room, her shoulders pulled back, her head high. Her simple black dress wasn't a showstopper like the designer gowns in the room, but it clung to her curves and emphasized her long legs. Simple and stunning. The last thing she wanted was for Adam to see her struggling. *I won't let him win.*

The guests had taken their seats when they returned to the ballroom, with the band playing an ambient piece. Ignoring the stares, Laura walked to her table. She took her seat with Mrs. Van Doren to her left. Across from her was an empty chair, reserved for Belinda's father. She stole a glance at Adam. It wasn't her imagination; he was definitely pretending he didn't see her.

How dare he act as if I don't exist?

Furious, she crumpled the napkin on her lap.

The celebrations began, but Laura couldn't focus. Adam's nonchalance bothered her. It hurt that he showed no remorse for breaking her heart. Belinda's grandfather, Howard Bancroft clinked his glass of champagne, capturing everyone's attention. He thanked everyone for coming to celebrate before launching into a sweet anecdote about Belinda from her childhood.

Laura's thoughts wandered until someone touched her arm. Glancing up, she met the wedding planner's expectant stare and the head of a microphone.

"Huh?"

"And now, to give a toast to our bride and her groom, Miss Laura Turner," The master of ceremonies called.

Oh, crap. Laura got to her feet with a shaky smile. She examined the crowd before her. Two hundred faces, extremely rich and entitled, staring back at her. Self-awareness took over. Her trembling hand reached for the wine glass. *I can do this. I won't panic. I can't let Belinda down.*

"Uh," she began. "I met Belinda during our second year in college. We don't have a lot in common, but, uh, I quickly found out we had similar taste in music...uh..."

What are you talking about? This is boring!

"Um..." she continued, bearing the painful silence from the crowd. "We also like having a good time. When she introduced me to Henry, I instantly knew that he was the one for her. They fit together like pieces of a puzzle. He was her rock and she, his anchor."

She glanced at Belinda who tearfully stared back at her.

"When I learned about their engagement, um..."

My boyfriend had just broken up with me.

"Uh, when I learned about their engagement—"

The back door opened, and a tall, dark-haired man entered, looking around.

Laura's voice trailed. Her fingers tightened around the microphone.

The man turned to the front of the room and their eyes met. He paused, his brows lifting. An ice-like sensation surged through her veins. With her mouth agape, she stared, willing her eyes to stop playing tricks.

Rob?

No way was this the man who'd secured a rent-free space in her head, making his way to the front of the room, staring like he'd never seen her before. He stopped at their table. He was real. Sexy, delicious looking, with his thick hair trimmed and wearing a tux that was made for him.

The master of ceremonies cleared his throat, bringing Laura back. *Crap.* The guests were waiting for the rest of her speech, but Rob's appearance had short-circuited her brain.

"Dad's here, thank God," Belinda mumbled, and Laura's head whipped around. Her stomach lurched as her best friend gave Rob a quick wave.

Huh?

Rob returned her wave before sinking into the reserved seat around her table.

Dad?

Oh, my God. I slept with Belinda's dad!

The tightening in her chest returned. Her head spun from a sudden wave of dizziness. The last thing she heard was Belinda's gasp as she fell to the floor.

·

Chapter 8

"Give her space. Belinda. Let her breathe. I'm sure she'll be alright."

Laura's eyes fluttered open and locked with a pair of worried gray eyes. Familiar eyes. Eyes that transported her back to Rome, back to the Trevi fountain and the allergy attack that almost took her life. She closed her eyes, immersed in the memory of the rushing water, the whispering of the people around her, a strong voice telling her that everything would be fine. She was at ease. This was a dream.

But another voice soon cut into her daydreaming. Belinda's voice. Her eyes flickered open, meeting Belinda's worried stare.

"Laura, oh my God, are you alright?"

Her best friend loomed over her, peering into her face. It took her a moment to realize it was Rob's strong arms cradling her frame. His scent washed over her, his body merged with hers, evoking the memories of him inside her. She eased away from him, and he let her go. Her body protested, already aching for more of his touch, but she ignored its carnal desire. There would be no touching Rob. Not anymore.

"Laura—"

"I'm fine, Belinda."

She looked around, taking in the small supply room. She remembered walking past it on her return from the powder room. *Who brought me in here? Was it Rob? Do I even want to know?*

"Are you okay?" Belinda helped her up. "You were out for like a few seconds. Should I call an ambulance?"

Laura shook her head, regaining her composure with a smile. "It's just a regular panic attack. I forgot to breathe, that's all."

She looked at her best friend, her face etched with stress from tonight's events, and then her eyes shifted to Rob. Side by side, it was easy to see their resemblance.

Fuck.

"I'm so sorry for ruining your evening," she said, taking Belinda's hand.

"Don't worry about it," Belinda reassured her. "Panic attacks are no joke. I shouldn't have put you on the spot like that. It's my fault, not yours." She took a napkin from her purse and dabbed Laura's forehead. "You should have seen the look on Mrs. Van Doren's face when you fainted. She dropped her martini glass," she ended with a chuckle.

Laura's face heated with embarrassment. "Oh no... I can't believe I fainted in front of Adam... and the Van Dorens... and the Rothchilds..."

"Screw them. To be honest, I think this right now, is the highlight of my engagement dinner."

Laura chuckled, but it wasn't a funny laugh. Being embarrassed among her peers was one thing. Passing out in front of the richest people in New York, well...

"Is there a back door out of this place?" she asked, and Belinda laughed.

"Come on, it wasn't that bad. They'll forget and move on within a few minutes." As if on cue, the band came alive with a snazzy selection. "See? I bet they are all making their way to the dance floor."

"Eh-em."

Laura glanced at Rob, their eyes meeting. His expression revealed nothing. Her racing heart confirmed her emotions were all over her face. She swallowed, breaking their eye-lock.

"Oh, Laura, let me introduce you to my Dad," Belinda said, taking Rob's arm. "Dad, this is my maid of honor, Laura Turner. Laura, meet my dad, Robert Wright."

"You have different last names," she blurted as Rob extended his hand.

"Um... Mother changed it after the divorce. Security reasons, she said." Belinda rolled her eyes and shook her head.

The discomfort of Belinda's face surprised her. Rob's expression was calm as the sea.

"It's nice to meet you, Laura."

The husky, erotic sound of his voice made her stomach flip. It was surreal being in the same room with him, knowing that two weeks ago, he was kissing her goodbye at an airport in Rome. She remembered his touch on her skin, how her lips curled when he kissed her, and how it felt lying next to him beneath the sheets.

She wiped her sweaty palm on her skirt before offering it. "Nice to meet you too, Mr. Wright."

The electric touch. It took her breath away.

"Thank God, Dad was there to scoop you up the minute you fell. You would think a bomb had just gone off the way Mom started freaking out. Such a drama queen," Belinda said with an eye roll.

"Thank you." Laura shook his hand.

"No problem," Rob mumbled, tightening his hold.

Oh no.

This is bad.

This is very, very bad.

Laura tugged her hand from his, her heart beating a mile a minute. She moved to a seat, gathering her thoughts as Belinda reunited with her Dad. She would give anything for this to be a dream, that the sex God who rocked her world wasn't the man across the room palming his daughter's cheeks.

Belinda can never know.

Laura's cheeks burned as she listened to Rob giving Belinda details on his trip. From visiting the Trevi fountain, having dinner at the finest restaurants, his mini tour around Rome and his drop in to see Antonio, but he conveniently failed to mention his date that night.

Me.

"Oh, wait. Laura just got back from Rome too. Such a coincidence," Belinda said, cutting in her thoughts.

A chill ran up Laura's spine and she feigned surprise. "Really? Yeah, definitely a coincidence."

"Still, it's so cool!" Belinda grinned, then turned to her dad. "Laura met some dreamy guy over there."

"Belinda!" *Is it too much to hope I was anywhere else right now?*

"Dreamy, you say?" Rob raised his eyebrows at her.

"He totally rocked her world. She's—what did you call it, Laura? —Dickmatized."

Oh, my God.

The wicked sparkle in Rob's eyes made her want to cover her face. "Nice," he murmured, capturing her stare.

"I'm just glad she got her groove back, after—"

"Belinda, please! I don't think your dad is interested in my love life," Laura said, wishing the earth would take her in. She threw her friend a desperate stare, and thankfully, Belinda caught the hint. She playfully drew a line across her lips.

Laura stole a glance at Rob. Then another. He looked amazing in that expensive tux, still with the rugged edge that made him sexy. The memory of his rough hands grazing her thighs, his fingers slipping inside her became so vivid, leaving a pit in her stomach.

She chanced another glance, and this time, Rob caught her. A silent agreement passed between them. Their Roman sex fest would remain a secret. No one could ever know, especially Belinda. Laura couldn't imagine her best friend's reaction if she found out. Their friendship would be over.

"We should head out," Rob said. "The guests must be wondering where you are."

"Before we go—" Belinda grabbed his arm. "—Since Laura is my maid of honor, I'm assigning her as your assistant, Dad."

Rob's brows lifted as Laura blurted, "Why?"

"To help him getting ready for the wedding and with whatever else he might need. He's too busy to remember it all."

"Correct me if I'm wrong, but that's not what a maid of honor does."

"Screw the status quo, Laura. It's my wedding. I make my own rules."

"What about Aubrey? She's more fashionable than I am."

"I already assigned her to assist Mom."

"I'll swap."

Belinda frowned. "Why? You can't stand my mom."

Laura's eyes darted to Rob then back to Belinda. "It's just that..." *I screwed your father, and I don't trust myself around him again.*

"Whatever it is, Laura, can you suck it up for me, please? I really need you."

"I can handle things on my own, Belinda. I don't need an assistant," Rob spoke up.

"You think you don't, Dad, but I promise, when you're eyeballs deep in work, you're going to need help getting things together. Laura's the most efficient person I know."

Rob's lips thinned, and an emotion flashed across his face, but it went by so fast Laura couldn't catch it. "Fine. I'll oblige." He wet his lips, lashing her with an intense stare that created an instant flashback to their last night in Rome; the luggage crashing to the floor as Rob cleared out the bed before placing her on top of it, settling between her thighs, his lips planting needy kisses on her neck as he unbuttoned her blouse. Wasting no time, he took her breast into his mouth, softly nibbling on her nipple, unzipping his pants with speed. She could still hear the thumping of the bed against the wall as he thrusted inside her and the loud, pleasurable moans that left her mouth.

"Laura?"

She snapped back to reality. "Huh?"

"Are you okay? Do you want to lie down on the couch? You zoned out for a bit," Belinda said, concerned.

"I'm fine." Rob's eyes were all over her, his hot gaze keeping the memories on the surface. Her hormones were biting at their restraints; how would she survive being alone with him?

"Okay, great. It's time to really head back," Belinda said, taking her father's arm.

Laura followed, absorbing the events of the night. Not only was her asshole ex pretending she didn't exist, but her lover was her best friend's dad. *This night can't get any worse.*

Julie approached them as they entered the ballroom, her flustered expression putting Laura on edge. *Maybe I talked too soon.*

"Is the theatrics over? Can our guests finally relax? The Rothschilds were about to leave. Thank God, Philip was charming enough to make them stay. Thanks for the drama, Laura."

"Julie, that's enough," Rob's deep voice filled in the silence.

"Oh, don't get me started, Mr. Late. Couldn't you show up on time for your only child?"

"Mom—"

"I showed up, didn't I?" Rob bit out, his expression tight. "Although, if you had your way, I wouldn't be here at all."

"Dad, please."

"Always one to cast blame, aren't you, Robert? Nothing's ever your fault. It's always been my doing."

"*Guys, come on!*" Belinda groaned. "Forget it. I'm going to find Henry." Without waiting for a reply, she cut through the crowd of dancing guests, leaving Laura standing awkwardly between Rob and Julie. The tension got worse when Adam joined them.

"I have to run, Julie. Duty calls. Thank you for inviting me. I'll see you at the wedding." Laura watched as he gave Julie a peck on the cheek, still ignoring her. She forced the fury aside.

"Oh, be a dear and send my regards to Victoria, would you?" Julie added, as Adam moved away.

Adam turned paper white but nodded. "Of course."

Who's Victoria? What is she talking about? Laura gaped as Adam walked away, leaving her yet again in the cold.

"Well..." Julie turned to Rob with a dry smile. "It's lovely seeing you, Robert."

"I can't say the same," Rob murmured, his dark frown worse than before. Watching their exchange, Laura made a mental note to ask Belinda about the divorce. What happened between them? She hadn't known Rob for long, but she'd never seen him so bitter.

Julie rolled her eyes before sauntering to a nearby group, leaving them alone. The reality didn't hit Laura until Rob turned to her and extended his arm.

"Can I have this dance?"

"Huh?"

The frown dissipated, and the ghost of a smile tugged the corners of his lips. "You heard me."

"That's not a good idea, Rob."

"It's just a dance. Think of it as me getting to know my assistant."

Laura huffed a breath, then reluctantly took his arm. Rob guided her to the dance floor and placed his hand on her hips. The hair on the back of her neck raised. She shifted her gaze to his chest. Bad idea. She placed her hand on his shoulder, and he took them into a steady rhythm.

"So," Laura began as they swayed to the music. "A daughter, huh? Shouldn't you have mentioned that during our first date?"

Rob chuckled. "I did say that, though."

"I thought you had a *child*," Laura insisted. "Like a ten-year-old or something."

"Does it matter?"

"Of course, it does! *You're my best friend's father*!"

Lower your voice, please," he said, glancing around. "It's not like I knew you were Belinda's best friend, Laura. We aren't the most social; I'd think you'd know that being her best friend."

"This is such a mess..."

"Is it?"

"Yes!" she hissed. "I fucked my best friend's father!"

Rob eyes darkened, and he wet his lips, stealing her attention. The urge to kiss him overwhelmed her. She gently tugged her hand, but Rob held his grip. "What are you doing?" he asked.

"I need to go." *Before these stupid hormones make me do something I'll regret.*

"Stay. The song isn't over yet."

"I can't—" She took a deep breath, realizing her departure would cause a scene. "Fine, but only until it's over."

"You need to relax."

"I am relaxed."

"I can feel the tension in your arms. Let go. If you're worried about Belinda discovering what we did, don't. What happened in Rome will stay there. Agreed?"

"Agreed." The drop in her stomach was a painful contradiction. *What if I don't want it to stay in Rome?*

"Good," Rob said. "How about we pretend we're just meeting for the first time?"

She smiled. "Fine by me."

"I'm Robert," he began, twirling her. "My friends call me Rob. You are?"

"Laura. Nice to meet you, Rob."

"Likewise."

They waltzed on the dance floor in silence until Laura opened with, "Can I ask a personal question?"

A brief apprehension crossed his face, but he gave her a nod. "Sure."

"Why don't you and Belinda share the same last name?"

"Now, that's *really* personal, Laura."

"I gave you a heads-up, didn't I?"

He dipped her, then took her for another spin. Laura figured he wouldn't reply until he mumbled, "It wasn't my doing, that's all I can say. You know how Julie is, so to avoid world war three, I allowed her to have that. That doesn't make Belinda less my child."

"Okay. Another question—"

"No. I'd prefer enjoying this dance without you probing in my head." His quick smile softened his harsh tone.

"I'm sorry."

"Don't apologize for being curious. You're not the first to ask me, anyway. Someday, I'll tell you all about it in more details. Maybe."

Someday? What does that even mean?

A waving hand caught her attention. It was Belinda, locked in Henry's arms, wearing a blissful smile. Laura waved back, a little guilty about the filthy thoughts that plagued her even now. Rob twirled her before taking her back into his arms once again. They toured around the dance floor with Laura trying not to enjoy it too much. She kept thinking about what Rob just said. What did he mean by it? Did he want to see her again?

No, he doesn't, and neither should you. Stop letting your emotions cloud your judgement, Laura.

What happened in Rome would remain a secret. She would only interact with him whenever Belinda needed her to. But as Rob pulled her against him, she couldn't help but long for the fantasy once again. The feeling of ecstasy, warmth, and being needed. The feeling of *him*.

I'm in trouble, aren't I?

Chapter 9

G*irls' Night*
An ambulance siren woke Laura from a deep slumber. After slipping on her glasses, she checked the time. It was six in the morning on a Saturday. She cursed the noise, but it was no use getting back to bed. Her eyes fell on the painting—Rob's gift— against the wall.

Lovers.

Laura's mind reeled as the memories of last night came rushing back. *Rob is Belinda's father. Oh, my God. I slept with my best friend's dad! What's worse, I should feel guilty about it, but I don't. In fact, I'd love to do it again.*

She groaned, palming her face. *I'm going to hell for this. I'm sure of it.*

Her stomach rumbled, reminding her of the food she'd passed on last night. She'd had no appetite, was too absorbed with trying not to let it slip that she had actually met Rob before. Luckily, Belinda remained clueless. Her best friend seemed too preoccupied to notice anything amiss.

After putting the kettle on to boil, she raided the fridge to make a sandwich. Her thoughts returned to Rob as she slapped a slice of cheese on whole wheat bread. They only had one dance, but it was enough to resurrect the passionate longing for him. It was wrong, so wrong, but there was no way to turn it off. A part of her didn't want to, either.

Belinda's request was a cruel twist of fate, a punishment for being spontaneous for the first time in her life. How would she handle being so close to Rob and wanting him so much?

God, I need you to turn these feelings off, please.

With a heavy sigh, she took her breakfast around the tiny kitchen counter. If only Rob was a younger man. If only he wasn't part of that stuck up, entitled world. Although, he didn't seem comfortable in that circle. Physically, he fit right in, but after assessing him last night, she noticed a slight uneasiness in his demeanor. She noticed he didn't mingle with the other guests, either.

Making a mental note to ask Belinda, she finished her breakfast and put the dirty plates in the washer. Graduation was in a few weeks. It was time to consider what she'd do next. There was no urge to find a 9-5 job; she wanted to follow her passion and paint. Sadly, it was difficult to get a foot inside the art industry without connections. She knew no one—

Rob.

Laura paused, her fingers still curled around the handle of the dishwasher. She knew Rob, and Rob knew Antonio. The artist had promised to assess her work. Should she remind Rob and ask him to help her out?

No. I won't ask him. Things are already weird between us. I'll find my own way.

Her cell phone beeped, and she immediately reached for the phone. It was a Facebook birthday notification. Adam's birthday. With an exaggerated eye roll, she deleted it. He'd been MIA for his entire birthday last year, leaving her sick with worry. He resurfaced a day later, claiming his friends had taken him on a surprise cruise, and he'd left his phone. She shouldn't have bought it then. Thinking back, she realized he'd been lying. He was with another woman. Victoria, probably. Adam's face turned white when Julie mentioned her last night. And it bothered Laura that she kept wondering who this mystery woman was. Adam didn't deserve another minute of her precious time.

Still, she tried racking her brain for any mention of the name in her conversations with Adam, but it never came up. She didn't remember any friends named Victoria, but it was obvious Adam knew her. The puzzle gnawed at her mind. The longer it lingered, the angrier she got. *Did Adam leave me for another woman? Really?*

Huffing a breath, she reached into the drawer for a pair of panties. *It doesn't matter anymore. He's not the one for me. I don't belong in his circle, anyway. I'll find a guy in my league, someone who won't try to change me. On the bright side, if he didn't break up with me, I wouldn't have experienced the best sex of my life.*

There's a silver lining to it, at least.

She was about to enter the bathroom when a knock came on the front door. She opened it without checking the peephole, then wished she had. Rob stood at the doorway, deliciously heart-stopping a navy t-shirt, faded jeans, boots, and his signature brown leather jacket. His spicy scent washed over her, making Laura aware she hadn't showered yet.

"What are you doing here?" she asked, feeling exposed in her T-shirt. Thank God it covered her thighs, especially since she had no panties on.

"I'm here for our appointment," Rob replied with a slight frown.

"What appointment?"

He sighed, reaching for his phone. "Belinda texted me an hour ago. She made a tux appointment at the bridal shop."

Laura groaned, remembering Belinda's instructions last night. Being a maid of honor meant biting off more than she could chew.

"Look, I'm only doing this to placate her, so if you're not up to it, I'll do it on my own," Rob said.

"Belinda will have my head if I don't show up, so, not a chance. Besides, she needs me to keep you in line. Apparently, you like pissing people off."

"Only the ones who deserve it," he replied, grinning.

A sudden creak across the hall caught Laura's attention. "Get in." She grabbed the front of his jacket and tugged him inside, shutting the door behind him. "Mrs. Kadinsky has a knack for gossip. I don't want to be a part of her storyline. Plus, Belinda comes here often. I don't want her to know you stopped by."

"Mrs. Kadinsky? The sweet old lady across the hall?"

"Oh no," she groaned. "She already saw you?"

"Even offered me iced tea."

"What?"

"Relax, she has no clue who I am. I don't understand, why are you so upset?"

"You're my best friend's father!" she cried. "You're *Belinda's dad.*"

"Indeed I am."

"Doesn't *any* of this faze you?" Frustrated, she ran her fingers through her hair.

"Just breathe, Laura. The last thing you need is another panic attack. This doesn't have to be complicated. It's a simple tux shopping and whatever else Belinda thinks I need help with. No one has to know we slept together. After the wedding, we can both move on."

Rob was right. It wasn't complicated. Once the wedding was over, they would say goodbye and pretend the other didn't exist.

"Fine. Let me shower, and we can be on our way." She gestured to the couch. "You can have a seat."

Rob moved toward it but stopped short when he saw the painting on the floor. His lips curled into a disapproving frown he directed to Laura.

"What, you didn't like my gift?"

Laura's face warmed as Rob reached for it and hung it on the wall. "Of course, I did. It was a nice gesture. Thank you."

"A nice gesture, she says," Rob mumbled, scoffing. "A nice gesture would be an invitation to have dinner. I don't buy expensive paintings for ..." He stopped himself mid-sentence.

Her stomach dipped as he moved closer. "Why did you buy it?"

"I saw how much you liked it, so I wanted to surprise you."

"Why?" The question came out in a whisper. She was suddenly aware of Rob's overwhelming presence in her tiny apartment. The urge to launch herself at him grew stronger by the second. She ignored the warning to back away. "Why?"

Rob's Adam's apple bobbed as he swallowed. "Do I need a reason?" His husky tone was laced with the same need that bubbled inside her. Laura took another step, relieved when he didn't move away.

"Yes. See..." Her trembling fingers traced the buttons on his shirt. "...I can't get you off my mind, Rob, and I need to know if the feeling's mutual." The sudden boldness was like a drug, intoxicating her, awakening the seductress inside her.

Rob released a loud breath, finally backing away. "My feelings aren't important, Laura. We both agreed this was a fling. The stakes are even higher than in Rome. We can't—"

"I understand." Rejection burned her throat, but she summoned a smile. "You're right. I don't know what I was thinking. Have a seat. I'll be back."

ROB WATCHED LAURA MOVING towards the bathroom and without thinking, he grabbed her hand. Emotions took over, stripping his self-control he had been battling since she opened the door. The thin material of her T-shirt kept her covered, but the telltale panty lines were missing. It was torture knowing she was naked under there. His fingers were itching to stroke her thighs, to sink inside her. He was a fool to think he could resist temptation. That he would just walk in here and pretend like he'd no longer burn for a woman he'd spent sleepless nights wishing he'd have again. He shouldn't have come here. It would have been safer to meet her downstairs, but he couldn't help himself.

Seeing her last night, discovering who she was gave him a mental trip like nothing else ever had. For weeks, he'd thought about her. He even toyed with seeing her again. He found her address within a heartbeat, but he couldn't bring himself to approach her. Instead, he tried to forget her.

Epic fail.

Now, it was even worse. Knowing she was his daughter's best friend did nothing to temper his need for her. In fact, he only wanted her more. Somehow the taboo invigorated him; almost like fire under his skin begging to be salvaged.

She stared up at him, her big, beautiful eyes piercing his soul. There was no way to resist that mesmerizing stare.

"I missed you," the words came rolling out his mouth.

"God, I missed you too," Laura whispered.

He cupped her cheeks, taking her mouth for a searing kiss that felt like coming home. Laura moaned, wrapping her arms around his neck, her body pressed against his, igniting him. With their lips still joined, Laura tugged at his jacket, and he shrugged it off, his lips moving downwards. Laura released a soft moan when he bit her nipple through the fabric, her grip tightening on his hair.

In one swift movement, he removed her T-shirt. Her fingers flew to undo his belt. His pants were at his feet within a second, and he'd barely stepped out of them when Laura tugged his boxers down.

"Mhm. Someone's in a hurry."

"Someone's hungry," Laura whispered against his mouth, kissing him. "You don't know how I've been longing for this."

"I can make an accurate guess," he teased, hissing as she fondled his cock. He gripped her wrist to pause her movement. "Before we proceed, Laura—"

"I know, this is just sex."

"You say it so casually, but I need to confirm that you're okay with this."

"I am. Trust me." She pressed herself against him. "Just fuck me, Rob. Please. Don't hold back"

Rob lifted her with a grunt, impaling her. Laura's mouth flew open with a sharp gasp as he braced her on the edge of the kitchen counter, burying himself to the hilt. He eased out with a shudder. The overwhelming sensation made him pause at the edge.

"Don't stop, Rob, please," Laura whimpered. "I need you."

With a gentle sigh, he pressed inside once more. Her pussy hugged him, pulling him all the way in, sending ripples of pleasure through him. He groaned, increasing his thrusts, enjoying the way Laura felt around him and basking in the reality of it. To think that just several days ago, he'd thought he'd never see her again – feel her.

He wanted to make the best of every moment and so did she. He wanted to thank the heavens for reuniting her with him again. With each thrust of his cock, he grunted, exploring every sweet and addicting inch of her pussy. She felt as tight as the last time and Rob filled himself with past memories as he fucked her. It was too good... like a drug even, and he prized himself on being able to have a woman like Laura in his arms. He clung to her, enjoying her whimpers as his cock explored her tightness. Her pussy constricted around him and it only urged Rob to go faster. He pulled her slipping body closer to the edge and rammed into her with a throaty grunt, burrowing inside her until he thought he'd lose his mind.

He pulled Laura down and made her to turn around. She gasped, her back turned to him, her ass jutted out to meet his thrusts. She gently rocked her hips from side to side as if hungry for what Rob was about to offer. It was one of his favorite positions to have her in and he was glad she was quickly getting the hang of it.

He used his cock to smear her juices all over her pussy, flicking it from top to bottom and teasing her entrance. Laura moaned and pushed her ass out even more, seemingly impatient to have him inside her. Rob aligned the tip with her entrance and pushed hard and deep, briefly closing his eyes as he slipped past her soft folds.

Laura moaned, thinking it always felt so overwhelming to be in such a position. Somehow, he felt bigger from the back and stronger and although she wanted to see his face, the anticipation drove her wild.

Rob smashed into her and her body shuddered with each thrust, her ass smacking against his pelvis. She leaned into the counter more, propping her elbows on the surface as Rob fucked her relentlessly. Well, she had asked for it and she was getting exactly what was asked. It was hard and rough – so much so that her pussy slightly burned from the onslaught and Laura knew she would be sore later, but she didn't mine. It would remind her of him when she left.

She bit her lips hard and closed her eyes tightly shut, her walls involuntarily gripping his cock as he fucked her.

"Oh fuck yes! Just like that, Rob!" she exclaimed between whimpers.

He slammed himself into her yet again and Laura lost herself, her hands slipping as her tits smashed against the cold counter. Rob crouched over her, grazing his teeth against her shoulders before he went to kiss her neck. Laura gasped, her knees slightly trembling as her orgasm began to beat at her gates.

"So fucking addicting, Laura," he whispered sternly, his voice husky.

His bucked, losing his rhythm and Laura gasped once more, her own orgasm setting in. She arrived at her peak just when a spurt of Rob's cum spilled into her.

She shuddered like a leaf in rain as she came, her body exhausted and humming with pleasure. Rob pulled out with a groan, unloading the rest of his seed on her reddened ass cheeks.

"Oh, fuck." Was it possible to feel satisfaction and regret at the same time? The emotion that ran through him seemed like a combination of both. Tearing his gaze from Laura – not wanting to make himself hard again – he reached for his clothes on the floor.

"Rob..."

He shook his head, still not facing her. "We should go; the faster we finish the better."

"Right." He glanced at her dry smile. "Got it."

Rob sighed. "Are you sure you're okay?"

"Of course." She turned to him smiling, but her eyes held no sparkle. "I'll be ready in a jiffy."

Rob watched her go, then he hauled on his clothes, kicking himself once more.

"SO, HOW WAS THE APPOINTMENT with Dad? Did he get under your skin?" Belinda asked, dropping on the couch beside Laura. She reached for a slice of pizza on the center table, then glanced at Laura with a frown. "Did you hear what I said—why is your face so red?"

"Uh— it's the spice, damn it. You went overboard with the crushed pepper."

"Sorry. Here—" She reached for Laura's glass. "—have some wine."

Laura took a sip as Belinda repeated, "How did the appointment go?"

"It was... fun." Not. Rob was so cool to her the entire time, only speaking when necessary. It puzzled her greatly. They'd just had the most sizzling sex, and there he was, pretending it didn't happen, that he didn't enjoy the heck out of it. Her center clenched as she recalled his sexy groans.

"Dad said the same thing, that he had fun. I'm relieved. Usually, he's not the easiest person to deal with. I'm glad he didn't give you a hard time."

Well, he gave me a hard something, Laura thought, her cheeks warming.

"There you are, getting all red again." Belinda closed the pizza box. "No more pizza."

Laura feigned a cough. "Yeah, definitely too spicy."

"According to Dad, he had a really good time, which proved I made the right decision putting you two together."

I beg to differ. This is the worst decision you've ever made.

"So... did you talk about me at all?" Belinda asked.

We didn't really do much talking. Laura's stomach churned as memories of their passionate morning filled her mind. Her butt pressing against the counter as he stroked her, the pleasure bursting inside her as she climaxed. Was it possible to be addicted to someone so soon?

"Earth to Laura."

"Huh?" The euphoria quickly subsided, replaced by an overwhelming guilt. Here she was, fantasizing about Rob with Belinda right beside her.

"Is he dating anyone?" Belinda asked.

"Why are you asking me? How should I know that?"

"I don't know." Belinda sighed. "I figured it would be easier for him to share things like that with people he doesn't really know. For small talk."

"Belinda, nobody talks about their dating life as small talk, especially to people they don't know. What does it matter who he's dating, anyway?"

Belinda shrugged. "I don't know... a part of me had always hoped my parents would get back together, especially since my mom and Philip are getting a divorce."

"Oh," Laura mumbled, her stomach falling. "But isn't Julie dating that French model?"

"Ugh. Don't remind me. It's disturbing. Crawford's only twenty. He can't even legally drink for God's sake!"

"I thought he was older than us."

"No, he's a fucking baby. And that's not even the worst part!" Belinda pushed to her feet, pacing, a dark scowl on her face. "She invited him to my wedding!"

"She did?"

"Yes!" Belinda shrieked. "And she's only known this guy for what, like a month? This is so typical of her! And not to mention, so fucking selfish! I don't want this guy at my wedding Laura, I barely even know him!"

"Have you tried talking her out of it?"

"Have you tried saying no to Julie Bancroft?" Belinda said. "That woman has never taken no for an answer in her life. It's even harder for me, since—" She sighed, palming her cheeks.

"Since what, Belinda?"

Sadness bathed her expression as she turned to Laura. "There's something I haven't told you. I'm the reason my parents got divorced."

"What?"

She sighed again. "I was fifteen when I caught Mom with Philip. Dad had left for a business trip to Europe. I got home early from a birthday party and caught them on the living room couch. I told Dad when he got back, and he filed for divorce a month later. Mom blamed me for breaking up the family. A part of me did, too. We were happy before I opened my big mouth."

"No, Belinda, you did the right thing. What your mom did was totally despicable." Her heart went out to Rob. Was this why he was so intense? Was he still harboring the hurt that Julie caused?

Is he still in love with her?

"I know that now, but I let her get inside my head."

Laura shook her head. Julie had always been bitchy, but manipulating her own daughter for a sin *she* committed was too much. "You need to stand up to her, Belinda."

"I wish I could."

"You can."

"How, when she's used to having her own way?"

"You allowed it, Belinda. Now, you can undo it. Stand up to her. Tell her no, for once."

"I'll try." Huffing a breath, she sank back to the couch, reaching for her phone. "I need to ask Dad about his plus one. I don't want him to bring some random bimbo to my wedding, especially if that bimbo can't even legally drink."

Well, it's different with us. I mean, I can drink.

It doesn't make a difference. If Belinda is this upset about her mother dating a younger man, how would she react if she finds out?

Laura twirled her glass. "What if the random bimbo makes your dad happy?"

"What?" Belinda twisted, her fingers hovering over the screen. "So he *is* dating someone?"

"No. I mean, hypothetically, *if* your father's dating a younger woman, would it matter, as long as she makes him happy?"

"I don't know, Laura," she sighed. "I don't know if I could ever accept it. There are plenty of women his age. Why would he date someone young enough to be his kid?"

"Would you disown him if he did?"

Belinda's brows lifted. "There's something you're not telling me. What is it?"

"I swear, it's just a hypothetical question."

"Laura, I swear, if I find out you're hiding something from me..."

"I'm not. I promise."

Yes, this was definitely a secret she would hold close to her heart.

Chapter 10

Laura flipped onto her back, staring at the phone screen hovering in her outstretched hand. She'd spent the last twenty minutes online, scrolling through Rob's social media pages. It was a stalker-ish thing to do, but like her fling with Rob would remain her little secret.

He was quite popular with women. Slender, leggy women, all tens, clinging to his arm in each photo, each obviously grateful for his attention. The green-eyed monster reared its ugly head. She quickly swiped past a photo with a gorgeous blonde, her fingers pressing too hard on the screen. She gasped as the red heart popped on the photo, then she quickly undid the action. Was Rob online? Would he notice she'd liked a photo of him with another woman?

Placing the phone on the carpet beside her, she glanced at Belinda snoring on the couch, her feet propped on the center table. *God, I'm the worst friend ever. If only I could turn off my feelings for him, but it's so hard.* Rising from the floor with a deep sigh, she headed to the bathroom to freshen up. As she washed her face, a sudden crash made her pause. Belinda's curse came right after, followed by another explosion, the sound resembling glass shattering against the wall.

"You asshole!" Belinda screamed. "Where the hell have you been?"

"For the last time, babe, my flight got delayed."

"Liar!"

The hell? Surprised, Laura stepped into the hallway.

"I checked your flight. You got in three hours ago, Henry. Stop lying to me."

"Babe—"

"Don't fucking touch me. Who is she?"

"Belinda, come on. There's no one else, you know that."

"Bullshit. You haven't touched me in weeks, Henry. You're fucking someone else, I just know it."

"Belinda— stop struggling, please. For the last time, I love you. Only you. Please, babe, believe me."

"I swear to God, Henry, if you're seeing someone else, I'll—" Belinda's words cut short as Laura entered the living room, the awkwardness stamped on her face.

"I'm sorry to interrupt guys. Let me grab my things and go."

Henry gave her a stiff smile before heading to the bedroom. Belinda ran her fingers through her hair with a frustrated sigh. "Sorry you had to hear that."

"Is everything okay, Belinda?"

Belinda shook her head. "No, but it will be, I promise."

"If you ever need to talk—"

"I won't. We're fine, Laura. This is a typical lovers' spat, that's all."

Laura nodded, though not convinced. "Can I help with anything?"

"I don't know, um..." She massaged her temples. "Can you check on my dad? See if he needs anything."

Oh, boy. "Sure thing," she replied. "Consider it done."

"Thanks, Laura. You're the best!"

Laura gave her friend a hug before leaving, keeping her smile in place until the elevator doors closed. She let out a sigh, leaning against the wall. The forbidden fruit kept dangling in front of her, pushing her towards the edge. *Can I keep my hands to myself?*

LAURA CLOSED THE APARTMENT door behind her, then reached for her cell phone. *Let's get this over with.* Taking a deep breath, she dialed Rob's number. He answered on the first ring.

"Wright speaking."

How was it possible to sound sexier over the phone? Laura's eyes fluttered shut. Instant swoon.

"Hello... who is this?"

Crap. "Um, it's Laura."

There was a pause, then a harsh sigh. "Laura, how did you get my number?"

"Belinda gave it to me. She wanted me to check if you needed anything."

Rob released a harsh sigh. "What I need is completely off-limits, so the answer is no."

Her stomach fluttered. *Does he mean what I think? Is he talking about me?* "Uh, okay then. Bye."

"Wait—"

"Yes?" *Tell me how much you need me, Rob, how you're struggling like I am.*

"My tux is still at the shop, but I'm too busy to get it. Have it delivered to my office, please."

Her heart crashed to the floor of her stomach. "Okay. Um... do I deliver it to you personally?"

"No, you may leave it in the lobby. My assistant will collect it."

His aloofness hurt, but it irritated her, too. She understood him wanting to keep his distance, but she didn't deserve this cold treatment. Without a reply, she jabbed the end button with a thumb, wishing he could feel the pain. *Asshole. I'm done pining over a man who doesn't want me.*

A TALL REDHEAD APPROACHED Laura as she entered the revolving glass doors of the luxury bridal shop. "Excuse me, are you lost?" she asked, her malicious eyes scanning Laura's figure. The faded jeans and plain T-shirt stuck out like a sore thumb in the luxurious space.

No, you prejudiced bitch. I was just here last week. "I'm here to pick up a tux for Mr. Robert Wright."

"Ah, yes." The woman's lips spread with a genuine smile. "Please wait here for a moment." After another slow-motion scan of Laura's outfit, she headed to a nearby room. Laura stood awkwardly in the middle of the store, her eyes wandering, checking out the space. A middle-aged woman was being fitted into a beautiful gown for an upcoming gala. On the other side of the room, there was a man returning a tux and demanding a refund. Behind him stood a tall, blond guy. A familiar guy. She recognized those broad shoulders anywhere.

Adam. The familiar fury rose. With a surprising surge of courage, Laura walked towards him, tapping on his shoulder.

"Fancy running into you here."

Adam turned, his face deathly pale. "Laura? Are you okay? What are you doing here?"

"Do I seem okay to you?" she whispered back. "What's going on, Adam? Why are you behaving so weird?"

"Adam? What's going on?"

Laura backed away as a blonde woman moved into their space, her deep frown directed at Adam. She was stunning, her thick blond hair sweeping her butt. Her blue eyes shifted, taking in Laura.

But Laura's attention wasn't on her face. The giant diamond ring on her left finger and the small baby bump sent shockwaves running through her body. It wasn't hard to connect the dots. Now, everything made sense.

"Adam, who's this?" the woman asked.

"No one, babe." He took the woman's elbows. "Come on, let's go."

But the woman didn't move. Her eyes were still locked on Laura.

"She seems a little angry for someone you don't know, doesn't she?"

"Victoria." Adam raised his hands. "I swear, I have no idea who she is."

"Oh, my God." Laura chuckled, finding her voice, the sound as dry as a bone. "You don't know me. Really. I was your girlfriend for two years, you asshole."

"What? Stop lying. Who put you up to this?" Adam replied, scoffing.

Laura's eyes widened. "Are you fucking kidding me, Adam? Really?"

"I think that's enough," Victoria said, glancing around. The entire store had paused, all eyes on them.

"Why are you doing this? Tell her you know me. Tell her!" Out of control, Laura grabbed Adam's shirt and shook him.

"Get off me!" He pushed her away. "You're crazy!"

"You're the one who's crazy, you piece of shit!" She gasped as large hands grabbed her from behind, pulling her back. "Were you fucking her when you were fucking me, huh?" she screamed as the burly security guard dragged her away. Humiliation washed over her. Not only did she not get the answers she was looking for, but Adam pretended he didn't know her *at all*.

She hailed a cab, sobbing as she climbed on to the backseat. She had never been this furious in her entire life. Ashamed. Her anger at Adam reduced her to a woman she didn't recognize.

Was that a wedding ring on Victoria's finger? Were they married?

No wonder Adam didn't give a reason for their breakup. He was already married to someone else, someone beautiful and wealthy.

Why wouldn't he? I never belonged in his world.

Mrs. Kadinsky's smile faded as she rushed past her. "What's wrong, dear?"

Laura shook her head, still sobbing, slamming the door behind her. She collapsed in bed, curling into a ball. *I'm not crying because I want him back. It's his rejection that hurts so bad. Add that to the fact he's been cheating while we were together. How could he do this to me?*

Her cell phone rang, cutting into her angry thoughts. Without checking, she pressed the answer button.

"Where are you?" Rob asked.

There was something about his clipped tone that opened the floodgates. Laura sucked in a breath, then burst into tears.

ROB PUSHED UP FROM his seat, alarm bells ringing, Laura's sobbing putting him on edge. "Laura, what's wrong? Did someone hurt you?"

Her incoherent response made him reach for his car keys and dash out the door. *God help whoever dared hurt a hair on her head. I'll fucking tear them from limb to limb.*

The possessive rage was a huge surprise. A huge, unwanted surprise. He didn't want this reaction to a woman he couldn't have. He was halfway to her apartment when it dawned on him. *Does Belinda know about us? Is that why Laura's crying so much?*

Ten minutes later, he pulled up to the curb in front of her apartment. Anxiety followed him upstairs. He blamed himself. He had been selfish, too caught up with wanting Laura that he hadn't reflected on how his decision would affect Belinda. He reached the second floor, still cursing himself. He'd never had to make considerations before. He and Laura weren't dating; who cared if they were having fun?

He reached her floor, wondering how he allowed himself to fall so deep. It should have been a fling that ended in Rome. He never expected to see her again. How could he have known she was Belinda's best friend?

You know now, Rob, yet you still messed around.

Sighing, he knocked on Laura's door. After a minute, she opened up, her eyes puffy under her glasses. She let him in and dropped onto the couch, tears streaming down her face.

"What happened?"

"She's pregnant."

"Who's pregnant?"

"His wife or whatever she is!" Laura cried. "That's why he fucking broke up with me!"

"Are you talking about Adam?"

"Yes!"

Rob swallowed hard and sat next to her while she sobbed into her pillow. It hurt to see her pained like this, yet he couldn't deny how relieved he was. She wasn't physically hurt, nor had Belinda discovered their secret. Small blessings. But at the same time, Laura was in shambles over another man. Regardless of the reason, Rob had never thought that it'd affect him like this, but there was a feeling of dread that loomed inside him, seeing her this way for a man she was obviously not over. Who was he kidding? He'd been delusional to think this was anything more than a fling for Laura – a way to get over her ex with good sex to distract herself.

Somehow the idea of that being true, tugged at something inside him, but he knew it was true. Still, he couldn't bear to see her like this and despite his reservations, his ultimate goal now was to comfort her in any way he could.

"He was fucking her while we were together, for God knows how long. And I was so stupid not to notice it at all! All those weekend golfing trips with his friends that *I* could never join because it's a boys' outing! What a joke!"

He stared, unsure of what to say or do.

She sucked in a breath, then another, her face a deep red. "And now they're married? When did that even happen? Was he really planning on breaking up with me? Or was he going to string me along like some delusional mistress?"

"Laura, I know you're upset, but you need to calm down—"

"Of course, I'm upset!" she shrieked. "I gave two years of my life to that man! I did everything I could to fit into his perfect little world! And this is what he gives me in return? He couldn't even have the guts to tell me the truth! What kind of a man is that?"

"That's a boy, not a man." Without thinking, Rob took her hand, giving it a gentle squeeze. "Laura, you deserve the world. You're a wonderful, amazing, and beautiful woman."

She scoffed, wiping her eyes. "This coming from a man who's been avoiding me like the plague."

"Our situation is different, Laura. You know that."

"I know, but it's hard remembering when my body wants you."

His pulse tripped. Blood rushed to his cock. He eased up from the couch and Laura followed, staring up at him with her bright, teary blue eyes.

"No one needs to know about us, Rob. It could be our little secret."

Rob released a harsh breath, tempted to give in. He experienced the same struggle Laura did. The battle between his body and mind was just as intense.

Seizing the advantage from his silence, Laura grabbed his collar and pulled him in for a deep kiss. With a regretful sigh, Rob eased her off.

"Laura, you're upset. I don't want to take advantage of a situation like this."

She tightened her grip. "You're not taking advantage of me, I promise."

"It's still not right." Still, he pulled her in for a tight hug. He caressed the back of her head as she laid on his chest. Wanting more, he placed a soft kiss on her forehead. His only aim was to drive the sadness away. At least, that was what he told himself. His body didn't agree.

"God, I wish I could escape for a while," she mumbled against his chest. "Just to get my head right."

"I have a place in the Hamptons," he blurted, against his better judgement. "I can give you the keys for the weekend. There's a private beach. A spa... everything you need for a relaxing time."

Laura eased from him with a smile. "Do you really mean that? It sounds like heaven."

"Of course, I do."

"I'd love to, but only on one condition."

Rob was afraid to ask, but he did anyway. "What is it?"

"I want you to come with me."

Chapter 11

Laura chuckled to herself as she entered the door to the bank. It was still hard to believe Rob had agreed to accompany her this weekend. It was an impulsive request, the words leaving her mouth without warning, not that she would stop them, anyway. She wanted him there with her. His unexpected reply was a pleasant surprise.

After handling her business, she left the bank, running into a pretty blonde who reminded her of Victoria. The memory of the unfortunate incident still left a bitter taste. Humiliation still burned her skin. She wasn't loud or violent. That vicious woman wasn't who she wanted to be.

Adam deserved to burn in hell for what he'd done to her. Instead, he got the happy ever after, the stunning prize, a family. It still hurt how he strung her along all those months when he had already moved on. The betrayal was more than enough for her to break down.

Why is life so unfair?

Fortunately, Rob was there for her last night; comforting, understanding, and never judgmental. He was a gentleman, too. He wanted her; the hard-on in his pants made that clear, but he didn't take advantage of her vulnerability. She was hysterical and wasn't thinking straight. He respected that. Another man would have taken advantage, but Rob wasn't just *any* other man.

If only he could be mine.

THE WEEKEND ARRIVED, and with it, a flurry of anxiety Laura had never experienced before. She didn't know what to expect from the mini staycation. Was it an intimate trip, or were they going as friends? The proximity would create sexual tension, for sure.

She checked the time. Rob was on his way, and she was still packing the things she needed to bring. Flustered, she opened her underwear drawer. Her stomach flipped as she stared at the flimsy red garment on top.

Should I bring those?

Sighing, she lifted the set of lingerie from her drawer. She'd bought it for her trip to Rome, but Adam had missed that window. She hesitated for a beat, then sheepishly stashed it into her overnight bag. Her phone rang as she pulled the zip close.

It was Belinda. *Damn it.* Taking a deep breath, she answered. "Hey, Belinda."

"Laura? Are you free tomorrow?"

The remaining excitement fizzled, replaced by an overwhelming guilt. *What should I tell her? Should I tell her the truth?* "Uh... I'm busy."

"Busy? On a Saturday? What are you up to?"

"Um... I'm going out of town, actually, my mom is...sick." It was a half lie, but still enough to make her feel bad. She hated lying to her friend.

"That sucks. I hope she gets better soon. Call me when you get back, okay? I'm having my dress altered on Monday."

"Monday? I thought it was the end of the month."

"It was, but Mom wants us to move the ceremony up a few weeks."

"What? Why? Won't your guests all be upset?"

"They'll understand."

"*I* don't understand, Belinda. Why the rush? You're barely out of college. Why are you in such a hurry?"

"There's no rush, Laura," Belinda said tightly. "I'm ready to marry Henry. Why wait?"

"Listen, I'm not trying to deter you. I hope you're making the right decision, that's all."

"I am, trust me. I have to go, okay? The wedding planner is here to discuss the changes we want to make. Call me when you get back, okay?

"Yeah," Laura replied. "I'll call you."

She hung up with an exasperated sigh and continued packing, despite the conflicting emotions. A knock sounded on the door as she zipped her bag, evoking a thrill. She opened it to Rob's warm, sexy smile.

THE SUN HAS ALREADY set when they arrived at Rob's beachfront property, a gorgeous contemporary home, large enough to house two families. After pressing his thumb against the front door to unlock it, Rob guided her inside. She stood in awe in the middle of the living room, taking in the huge space. It contained two sectional couches with a coffee table between them, a large TV above the fireplace, and stunning art on the walls. Floor to ceiling glass doors gave them a spectacular view of the beach. She turned to face him with a smile. "Cool place you have here."

"Thanks. I bought it when my company took off. It was my first real estate investment."

She nodded, removing her coat and dropping into the couch with a soft thud, already at home. Rob smiled at the sight of her head tossed back, her arms outstretched, and her eyes closed. It must have been a difficult week for her. He didn't find it easy too. Resisting his urge for Laura was the hardest thing he'd ever done.

"How are you doing?" Rob asked, sitting next to her.

Laura opened her eyes, leaning on her arm in a tilted position, her hair spilling over her shoulders. Her dark top brought out the electric blue in her eyes. As she bathed in the warm glow of the fire, he couldn't help but think how perfect she looked. Spending the weekend with Laura was the last thing he expected, but it was hard to say no when she lashed him with those big, gorgeous eyes.

She smiled. "It's getting better, now that I'm away from it all."

God, that smile of hers. He was very tempted to kiss her, but he held back. Mixed emotions raged inside him. His feelings for Laura were unlike anything he'd ever felt before. He was at home around her. The way they clicked made her irresistible. A part of him wanted to continue their fling, but his conscience was busy working overtime. He didn't want to ruin her for other men.

Other men... fuck. Just the thought of another man touching her made him want to punch a wall.

"What are you thinking about?" she asked.

"You," he whispered.

He was slipping, aching to be inside the fantasy once more. He slowly leaned into her and gently kissed her lips. Laura kissed him back. She pushed against him, harder and stronger this time. It was almost as if she'd held back all this time, and now she finally learned to let go. Back in the city, he was always walking on eggshells, worried that their secret would come to light. Here, surrounded by the privacy of his beachside home, there was no holding back.

Rob deepened the kiss, cradling the side of her face with his warm hand. She felt cool to the touch, but the red tinge on her cheeks betrayed how aroused she was. He slipped his tongue inside her mouth, and she opened for him, her soft moan hardening his cock. She wrapped her arms around his neck. Rob dipped under her shirt and unclasped her bra. He took her firm breasts into his hand and squeezed them. Laura hissed, the sound like music to his ears.

They broke their kiss for air, but there was no time to waste. He longed for her. The hunger was too much to bear. He wanted to feel her hot body once again. He grabbed her waist, moving her onto his lap, then removing her shirt. With her chest exposed, he was now free to feast on her nipples. He took one in his mouth, gently sucking while tweaking the other. She let out moans of pleasure, grinding on his lap, her fingers undoing his belt. Shifting her to the couch, he tugged the waist of her pants, and she lifted her hips to get them off, revealing sexy thong panties that made his mouth water.

"I want you," she moaned.

Rob trailed his kisses down her torso and gripped the thongs with his teeth. He pulled it down with his mouth, revealing her dripping center before him. He'd already lost the fight. There was no more resistance left in him.

Laura straddled him once more, grazing her sex against his tip. Rob let out a loud groan, already halfway to heaven. With her hand on his cock, she slowly slipped it in, taking his full length, moaning. Her sexy sounds drove him crazy. He grabbed her hips and buried himself inside of her. Laura screamed a full release of pleasure and grabbed his hair.

"Fuck," Rob groaned.

He moved inside her, knifing upwards. She panted above him, her breasts bouncing as she enjoyed the ride. Her fingers gripped his back, her nails marking his skin. He kept the rhythm, enjoying the sound of his skin slapping against her ass. Laura embraced him, her chin resting on his shoulder.

"I'm coming!" she screamed.

Rob picked up the pace, his sweat mixing with hers, their breaths mingling as her sex pulsed around him. He tightened his grip on her ass, joining her in climax. Laura descended from her high, settling her head on the crook of his neck. Rob kissed her shoulders and brushed the hair away from her face.

"We're not done yet."

He was still hard, still wanting even more of her. A heart-stopping thought made his grip tighten around her. *I will never get enough.*

Chapter 12

Rob's eyes fluttered open, the irresistible scent of frying bacon wafting past his nose. He got out of bed, finding Laura over the stove wearing his shirt from the night before and nothing beneath. She jumped when he surprised her with a hug from behind.

"Breakfast?" she offered.

"Sure, I have my breakfast right here." He kissed the back of her neck, and she giggled. She placed the bacon and eggs on the counter and turned off the stove.

"Fire hazard," he smirks.

"You're a hazard," she replied, giggling. She turned to face him, her back resting against the counter. She pulled him in closer and kissed him.

"Hungry?"

"Not for food," Rob murmured. He grabbed her hair, pulling it back for a view of her neck. His lips trailed kisses to her collarbone as he unbuttoned the shirt, leaving her breasts exposed.

"Mmmm..." Laura moaned as he sucked on her nipple. His hand traveled below, cupping her bare sex, pleased to feel she was already wet. He slowly rubbed her clit in a swirling motion, watching the hunger settle within her eyes before they snapped shut. Lifting her, he placed her on the counter and settled between her legs, pressing inside with a swift thrust. Laura gasped, clutching his arms, her walls tightening around his thick, hard length. She angled her hips to receive more of him. His ass clenched as picked up the pace. Her breasts bounced from the motion, tempting his lips once again. He dipped his head and sucked on the erect bud. She let out a scream of pleasure, digging her fingers into his back.

121

"Oh, god, oh god," Laura whispered. "Don't stop!"

Rob obeyed her command, thrusting deeper, and from her sensual whimpers, knew he'd hit her sensitive spot. He brought her to the bed afterwards, curling up with her. He brushed the damp hair away from her face and kissed her forehead, the rush of affection taking him by surprise.

Careful, Rob. You just might fall for this girl.

"I think I'm full," Laura murmured, peering up at him. "There's no need for breakfast anymore."

Rob chuckled in reply, pulling her closer, contentment washing over him. *Don't worry,* he responded to the warning bells*, I promise I won't fall.*

AFTER A NAP, THEY DIVED into brunch. Rob cooked up pancakes while Laura made a fresh batch of eggs and bacon.

"It's been a while since I've done this," Rob commented as they sat around the dining table.

"Done what?" Laura asked.

"Had a sit-down meal with someone in my home," he replied. "Usually, I'm alone."

"How come? I mean, based on your social media activity, you seem like a popular man—" Her eyes widened, and she clasped her mouth. Rob chuckled.

"In case you're wondering, I did catch that like on my profile." He laughed even more as her face went beet red.

"I swear, I'm not a stalker or anything. I was just browsing."

"If you say so. I'm flattered, anyway."

She scoffed. "I would find that easier to believe if I hadn't seen those beautiful women on your arm."

"They're nothing compared to you; trust me."

Again, that overwhelming blush. "And you're too generous."

"I'm being truthful, Laura. When was the last time you really looked in the mirror?"

"This morning."

"I mean, really looked. You're stunning, and it's not just the outer layer. I wish you would see that."

"You barely know me. How can you say that?"

"I know enough to determine what's true and real."

Her cheeks went crimson once more, and her head dipped as she placed a piece of egg in her mouth. "I've never met a guy who made me feel this good about myself," she said.

"You've been searching in the wrong places."

She smiled at him. "I agree."

A beat passed as their eyes locked, both too entranced to look away.

"Why do you eat alone at home?" Laura asked after losing the stare-down.

Rob shrugged. "I haven't found someone... worthy of such intimacy."

"It's just eating, Rob, not settling down," she replied with a faint smile.

"It's not just food, not to me. It's allowing someone in my personal space."

"Why is that such a big deal? Don't get me wrong. I'm not trying to disregard your preference. It's just... unusual."

"I'd rather not say." He smiled to soften his stiff tone. "I'd rather talk about you. What are your plans after graduation?"

Laura shook her head. "I'm still on the fence about my next step. I'd love to pursue an art career, but I need a sustainable job to pay my bills."

"Why didn't you study art?" Rob asked. "They've got good schools in New York."

Laura shrugged. "Mom didn't want me to. Besides, I didn't think my work was good enough."

"Is that your opinion or your ex's?"

"It wasn't just Adam. I love my mom to death, but she's not the most supportive person I know. She pushed me to study business instead, said art was just a hobby, not a career."

"Well, you've met Antonio. You know that's not true."

"He's been such an inspiration," she gushed. "I'd love to follow in his footsteps someday."

"I'm sure you will." Rob smiled. "I think you've got what it takes."

Laura's head dipped, hiding the pleasure on her face. She fiddled with the food on her plate before looking back at him. "Can we have dinner on the pier? As much as I love hanging out in this beautiful space, I'm longing for the outdoors."

"Uh..." Leaving the house wasn't part of his plan, but Laura had never been to the Hamptons. He didn't want to deny her a good time. "Fine. As long as we remain discreet."

A part of him wished they didn't. Deep inside, there was a longing for more than this secret affair. He wanted to hold her hand in public, to kiss her on the streets, to show her off to the world. He shook his head. *This is crazy. What happened to fucking without emotions, Rob? You promised not to cross that line, remember?*

He sighed as Laura nodded gleefully. "I'm the queen of discretion. Don't worry."

"Good, because I know a special place."

THE PIER WAS FILLED with people wanting to witness the sunset. Rob and Laura moved through the crowd, careful not to appear too intimate.

"I could get enraptured in a place like this," Laura said, staring at the horizon with awe.

"Wait until dinner. One taste, and you'll never want to leave."

"I already don't want to." She directed her smile at him, but it faded as she caught herself.

They stopped at a quaint seafood restaurant on the far end of the pier. Rob specifically asked for a corner table and the hostess led them to a booth with a view of the ocean and the privacy Rob needed. The restaurant was empty, anyway.

"Did I tell you how stunning you look in that dress?" Rob commented as they sat down. The off-shoulder red dress made her beautiful complexion glow.

Laura blushed. "Only about five times, you flatterer. You're not too bad yourself."

Rob glanced down at the simple sweater and tailored pants he'd worn. "Now, who's the flatterer?"

"I mean it. You look good."

He smiled, reaching for the menu. "I hope you like it here. It's one of my favorite places."

"It's already one of my favorites."

"Oh, is that so?"

"Yeah, because you're here with me."

Taking a risk, Rob reached for her hand, bringing it to his lips for a kiss. "You have a way with words, you know that?"

"Only around you." She squeezed his hand as he released her. "Thanks for saying yes to this weekend. I didn't want to be alone."

"You didn't give me a choice anyway, with those big, beautiful, puppy dog eyes."

She grinned. "I don't know what you're talking about."

He chuckled. His eyes dipped to the table as she ran her foot up his leg.

"Want to hear a secret?" she asked.

"Sure."

She leaned in slowly and whispered, "I'm not wearing any panties."

Oh, fuck. Rob eyes flew shut. Add an instant hard-on to the list of things he wanted to hide. The only thought on his mind was her nakedness under that dress.

"What, nothing?" she asked.

He released a harsh sigh. "Laura, you don't know how much I want to rip you out of that dress right now."

Her expression darkened, and she blew out a breath. "I'm so looking forward to that."

"YOU'RE RIGHT. THAT was the best calamari salad I'd ever tasted," Laura said as they walked from the restaurant. She'd slipped her arm through his, and for once, he didn't resist. He was too upbeat, too... content. Yes, that was it. Extremely content. Why did it take a woman half his age to make him feel like this? Worse, his daughter's best friend. Any other woman would do. But she was the only one who did.

"Robert, is that you?"

Rob turned toward the thin, familiar voice, and the blood drained from his face.

Fuck it to hell. He quickly disentangled his arm from Laura's.

Of all the persons to run into... fucking Crawford Shultz, Julie's boy toy. He'd met the asshole once, and he instantly suspected the younger man's interest in his ex-wife. He'd seen the women Crawford previously dated; they were all in his age group. There was no doubt he was using Julie for her connections. Not his business. She deserved it, anyway.

"How's it going, Crawford?" he managed, forcing a smile, but Crawford's eyes weren't on him. Rob's heart sank as he took Laura in. From her stiffened stance, she realized they were busted, too.

Oh, shit.

"It's going," Crawford replied, still staring at Laura. "Do I know you from somewhere?" he asked her.

"I don't think so. I've never met you before." Rob hoped Crawford didn't notice the light tremor in her tone.

"Oh, you look like someone I've seen before. Then again, we all have a doppelgänger, don't we?" Crawford chuckled.

"It was nice running into you, Crawford, but we must get going." Without waiting for a reply, he hurried Laura away, picking up speed once they reached the end of the pier.

"Wait a minute," Laura huffed, jogging to keep up with him. "What's the rush? He doesn't know who I am."

"Are you kidding me? Laura, he's not an idiot. It will take nothing for him to connect the dots, especially if he attends Belinda's wedding."

"Oh, shit." Laura stopped short, slapping her forehead. "I never thought of that."

"Well, we need a plausible explanation if he runs his mouth." He rushed off, Laura still trying to keep up with him.

"How about the truth—hey, can you slow down?"

He paused, whirling on her. "You're joking, right?"

"Would it be so terrible if it gets out? Rob, we're two consenting adults."

"Only *I'm* trying to repair the relationship with my daughter. I have something to lose. You obviously don't."

"That's not true. The difference is, I care enough about you to take that risk."

Rob sighed. His conscience awakened, lashing him with an I-told-you-so. Damn it. Why didn't he listen? Why the hell did he touch her again and again? He shouldn't have come, shouldn't have said yes. Now, he'd dug a deep hole with no way out.

"That awkward silence tells me everything I need to know," she said, moving past him. He sighed, allowing her to go. His eyes closed in beat with the slamming of the front door as she stormed into the house.

Time to finally nip this in the bud.

GOD, I'M SO STUPID, Laura thought, *wiping her teary eyes. Why did I think Rob wanted more than sex? Why did I allow myself to fall for him?*

Crossing her legs before the fireplace, she settled the glass of wine on the floor and wrapped the blanket around her. *My anger is misplaced; this isn't Rob's fault. He promised me nothing but a good time, and he delivered one hundred percent. It was my weakness that got in the way.*

The front door opened, but she didn't turn to look. Rob's heavy footsteps came towards her at once. He stopped beside her, and for a moment said nothing.

"Penny for your thoughts."

Trust me, you don't want to know. "Do you think Crawford will tell Julie about running into you?" It was a safer topic, disheartening as it was.

Rob shook his head, but his expression seemed tentative. "Probably not, who knows? You've never met him before, so I'm not even sure it's something he'll mention to Julie."

"What if he did? Do you think Julie would tell Belinda?"

Rob scoffed. "No. Knowing her like I do, she'll hold that information over my head for a long-time, probably blackmail me, too."

"That's terrible."

"That's mild, compared to everything she's done. That woman is..." he shook his head. "She's different and not in a good way."

"Belinda told me how much she wanted you guys back together. Has she ever mentioned it to you?"

Another scoff. "She wouldn't, not when she knows how I detest her mom."

Laura grimaced. "She also told me what Julie did to you."

Rob's face darkened, his shoulders straightening. "She had no right."

"I—" *Damn it, I probably shouldn't have opened my big mouth.* "Don't tell her I said anything, okay?"

He walked away with a huff. Laura pushed to her feet, hurrying after him. "Is that why you've been single all this time? Are you afraid of getting hurt again?"

Rob shook his head. "My emotions are none of your business, Laura."

Ouch.

He caught the embarrassment on her face and sighed. "I'm sorry. Things are just complicated." He removed a cigarette from the pack and lit it.

"It doesn't have to be, you know," she said.

Rob took a deep draw, the frustration on his face triggering a drop in her stomach. "Laura, I really like you a lot, but you're too young to —"

"Too young?" Laura scoffed. "Where was that opinion when you were fucking me last night?"

"I could fucking kick myself," he mumbled.

"What does that mean?"

"It means I shouldn't have touched you. Not in Rome and certainly not here. You're definitely too young. Immature. You can't handle a man like me."

"I can't—" she shook her head. "It's funny how you never thought of this before."

"Laura, listen—"

"Just forget it." She turned and walked toward the fireplace, her glass of wine still on hand. She took a big gulp and exhaled, willing her self-control to return. She didn't want to appear like a nagging, needy girlfriend.

"I don't understand what you're asking of me," Rob said, his voice right behind her. "We were both aware this is just a fling."

She turned to him. "Do you think this could ever be more than a fling?"

"Laura..." He sighed.

His resigned expression was like a stab in her heart. She bit her lower lip, the tears forming under her eyes.

"God, Laura, come on..."

"It's fine. Just say the words, put me out of my misery."

Rob released a long, sharp exhale. "I can't give you more than sex, Laura. It's time for us to end this. I don't want to hurt you anymore."

She nodded, the tears spilling down her cheeks. He moved toward her, but she fanned him away. "Don't touch me, please."

"Laura—"

"I'm fine." She headed to the bedroom and closed the door, sobbing as she fell onto the bed.

Chapter 13

God, I really don't want to be here.

Laura stood before Belinda's apartment building, contemplating whether to turn around. This was the last place she wanted to be, considering how heartbroken she was. Being around Belinda would remind her of Rob's rejection, and she didn't want to think of that right now. She couldn't chicken out, though. Belinda needed her, and as the maid of honor, it was her duty to show up whenever the bride wanted.

Daniel, the doorman, opened up with a huge smile that Belinda quickly returned before stepping into the lavish lobby. She hadn't smiled since Saturday night, not even a chuckle. It was if the cheerfulness had evaporated from the world.

She hadn't spoken to Rob since he cut their Hamptons trip short and dropped her home, and she didn't expect to, either. He made it clear he wanted nothing to do with her. The feeling was mutual.

Lies...

"Okay, fine," Laura whispered to herself as she pressed the number for Belinda's floor. "I don't feel the same, but I really wish I did."

The elevator doors opened to Belinda's suite and a flurry of activity in the living room. Belinda's bridesmaids were already there. So was Julie. Laura resisted the urge to roll her eyes.

"Laura! You're here! Thank God. I was just about to try on the dress."

"It's already here?"

"What do you think? I've been up since six in the morning waiting for everyone to arrive! I can't believe my dad beat you here, and he's always late."

Laura's stomach dropped. "Your dad?"

As if on cue, Rob appeared from the hallway, his eyes briefly sweeping over Laura before settling on the artwork over her head. "Laura, good seeing you," he said with a nod.

"Hello, Robert." It was so painful seeing him, but she forced a slight smile.

"Okay, enough with the pleasantries. I'm going to try on my dress." Belinda said, rushing into the bedroom with an excited squeal.

Laura took a seat in the farthest couch from everyone, away from Belinda's salty bridesmaids, Julie's disapproving frown, and Rob's obvious attempt to pretend she wasn't in the room. It hurt like hell, but in half an hour, she would return to the safety of her apartment to continue licking her wounds.

"So," Julie began, her cool eyes taking Laura in. "How was your weekend, Laura?"

"Huh?" Julie was never interested in her life. Why now?

"Your weekend, dear. How was it?"

"Um..., it was fine. I've been busy sending out job applications."

"Oh?" Julie raised her eyebrows. "Wasn't your mom sick? Belinda told me. She wanted to invite you over to dinner last Saturday night too."

Laura sighed inwardly, giving herself a mental slap. "Ah, that's right," Yeah, she's doing better now."

"I bet." Julie smiled, turning to Rob. "And how was *your* business trip, Robert?"

What the hell?

Rob's expression gave nothing away as he replied. "It was okay. Nothing worth mentioning."

Laura's stomach dipped.

"Oh, but it must have been important for you to miss dinner with your future in-laws," Julie said.

Rob sighed. "Julie, let's not to do this right now."

Julie crossed her legs, a smirk on her face. "I feel like taking a trip when this wedding is over. The Hamptons sounds good. Crawford was there last weekend. He told me how he ran into a couple who've been keeping their affair on the downlow. It will create such a scandal if it gets out."

The walls closed in, stealing Laura's breath. *Oh, my God. She knows.*

"Oooh, Aunt Julie, tell us more!" Gina, Belinda's cousin spoke up. "Who are they?"

"Hush, now, Gina. I'm sure they wouldn't want their secret being talked about. No one likes being the center of such a debacle, do they, Rob?"

"I'm sure they don't," he replied, frowning darkly at her.

She seemed oblivious to his warning, instead turning to Laura. "Have you ever been to the Hamptons, dear? It's such a beautiful place."

Laura's breath caught in her throat. "Uh—"

"Voila!"

Belinda bounced into the room in the snow-white ball gown, straight from a fairytale storybook with a sweetheart neckline and yards and yards of tulle. The cathedral veil swept behind her, running like a waterfall to the end of the hall. She twirled, her arms extended to each side. "What do you think?"

"You look wonderful darling," Rob smiled, giving her a peck on the cheek.

"Perfect, *just* perfect!" Julie clapped her hands. "The most beautiful bride in New York!"

"No, the entire country!" Gina chipped in, and Laura didn't hold back the eye roll this time. *Kiss ass.*

"Well, what do you think Laura?" Belinda asked, when she said nothing.

"You look stunning, Belinda, as always."

"Do you think the veil is too much?"

"It's perfect," Julie chipped in before Laura replied. "What does Laura know about fashion, anyway?"

"Mom!"

"What?"

Laura stood, reaching for her bag and left for the bathroom. She didn't have to go, but she couldn't stand being in the same room as Rob and Julie, especially with Julie knowing what happened last weekend.

I'm so fucking stupid! Of course, Crawford would tell her! God, Belinda's going to hate me for this.

Taking a deep breath, she splashed water on her face. The pounding of her heart was like a bass drum in her ears. Julie had never liked her and Belinda's friendship. Laura wasn't from the upper class; she didn't fit the image of the friends Julie wanted around Belinda. There was no doubt she would use the opportunity to break them apart.

What can I do to stop her? I can't lose my only real friend.

The bathroom door opened as she reached for the towel to wipe her face. Startled, she whipped around to meet Julie's menacing stare.

"In case you missed the subtle hints I've been throwing out there, let me make it clear. I know you've been sleeping with my husband. You have some nerve, you little sneak."

"What are you talking about?"

Julie crossed her arms. "Don't give me that innocent look. You're not fooling me. Others may think you're some virginal reinvention of every guy's wet dream, but I know you're just a little whore."

"I'm not a whore, and Rob's not your husband. Not anymore."

"Honey..." Julie laughed with an air of sarcasm. "We might not be together on paper, but everyone here knows the rules. You obviously don't. You could have any man you wanted in New York, Laura, but you just had to dip your toes in the forbidden pool, didn't you? Belinda's dad, really?"

"I didn't know he was Belinda's dad when we met in Rome, okay? If I did, I would—"

"Fuck him again, which you did. It didn't end in Rome. You continued your little love affair here, too. This city has eyes and ears, Laura. I know what you two have been doing. Don't think you can get anything past me." Julie shook her head disapprovingly. "Do you know how much this will hurt Belinda?

"Please don't tell her." Her voice was broken

"Doesn't she deserve to know?"

"No, not like this," Laura insisted. "I swear, it's done. Rob and I are completely over."

"Rob?" Julie's brows lifted. "How fucking cute. I'm not surprised, though, I always knew you were a little homewrecker. I heard about your fight with Adam at the bridal shop. Pathetic."

Tears filled Laura's eyes but she wouldn't dare let them fall. "Why do you hate me so much?"

Julie sneered, obviously enjoying Laura's pain. "You don't belong here. Never did. It's time for Belinda to realize it, too." She laughed as she meandered her way back to join the others. Laura stood there shaking, trying to process all that had happened. Her throat was constricted and she wanted to bawl her eyes out, but she'd spent enough time feeling sorry for herself. That time was over.

Belinda had already returned to the bedroom to remove her wedding dress, so Laura didn't wait. Ignoring Rob's confused stare, she dashed out the front door.

LAURA STEPPED FROM the elevator into her apartment building, running into the last person she expected to see. She arranged the dirtiest expression and moved forward. "What are you doing here?"

Victoria stood stiffly by her apartment door, her delicate hands holding a tiny designer purse. She wore a cute, flirty dress that emphasized her baby bump. On her feet were simple strapped sandals.

"We need to talk," Victoria replied, her tone as hard as her face.

Laura moved past her, slipping her key into the door. "I can't imagine why."

"You know my husband. I want to know how."

"I'm sure you're not stupid. You heard the fight with me and Adam that day. Figure it out." She attempted to close the door, but Victoria restrained it with surprising strength.

"Look, I'm not here to fight."

"Then *why* did you come here?"

"Because." She hesitated for a beat. "Adam insists that he doesn't know you, but I know better. I saw the panic on his face. He's my husband. I know when he's hiding something from me. I just need the details, please."

"When did you get married?"

Victoria's brows lifted. "Does it matter?"

"To me, yes."

"A month ago."

Around the time he broke up with me. Asshole.

Sighing, she stood aside and allowed Victoria to enter, gesturing to the couch. "How long were you together?"

"About a year. We didn't plan this pregnancy, by the way. When my parents found out, we had to get married right away. But I know he loves me. I can't believe he's been unfaithful to me."

Laura shook her head. The entire time she thought Adam loved *her*, he had been seeing someone else all along. The worst part was, Victoria didn't know there was another woman involved. If anything, she was also a victim in this mess.

She sighed. "Victoria, I don't know how to tell you this."

"Tell me what?"

"Adam and I were together for two years. We broke up around the same time you got married."

Victoria clutched her necklace with a comical effect Laura would have found funny, if not for the terror on her face.

"Two years? That's not possible," Victoria whispered.

"It's true." She moved to her closet and removed a few outfits Adam had left. She had intended to throw them out, but luckily, she didn't. They were proof she was telling the truth.

Victoria gasped, lifting a red sweater from the pile. "I bought this for his birthday last year."

"He told me it was a gift from his mom."

Victoria shook her head, clutching the sweater in her arms. "How did he break up with you? What did he say?"

"He booked us a weekend in Rome, but he didn't show. When I landed, he broke up with me on the phone. He said he would always love me, but this is something he had to do."

"What did he mean by that?"

"I don't know... I assumed he was being forced to break up with me, but—" she caught the alarm on Victoria's face. "I'm sure that's not true."

"Oh, my God." Victoria moaned, returning the sweater to the heap.

"Look, I'm sorry this is happening to you."

Why are you apologizing?

"I don't need your pity!" Victoria screamed. She clutched her stomach, giving Laura a sharp glare. "And I don't care if you slept with him for two years. That means nothing."

"Why are you flipping on me? He played us both, Victoria. I'm a victim, too."

"You're no victim. You're a homewrecker. If you go near my husband again, I swear—"

The hell? Being called a homewrecker twice in one day didn't sit well with Laura. She marched to the front door. "Get the fuck out of my apartment you stupid bitch!."

Victoria gasped, clearly taken by surprise. But then she lifted her head high and moved towards Laura. "Consider this your closure Laura because you're never going to see him again."

"Not that I fucking want to. You and Adam can rot in hell for all I care. I'm over you people." She slammed the door, cutting Victoria's reply. She went to work, removing Adam's clothes, tossing them into a box. It was time for a purge, time to completely remove Adam from her life. She had been too distracted by her feelings for Rob to erase all the physical memories of him.

It was all a facade. Adam had never wanted her. She never met his standards, and she would've never been good enough, no matter how she tried. She dodged a bullet right there. But the fury still raged inside her.

Son of a bitch. Did he take Victoria to that corner cafe where they had their first kiss? Did he take her ice skating in Central Park, where he said I love you for the first time? When Adam curled up next to Victoria in bed, did he kiss her shoulder—

It doesn't matter anymore, Laura. You're over him. Release the anger and move on.

She sighed, her eyes landing on the painting sitting on the wall. *Lovers, my ass.* Rolling her eyes, she removed it, then turned it face down on the floor.

Men. They are nothing but assholes through and through.

Chapter 14

"What did you say to Laura?" Rob asked Julie as Belinda left to meet with Henry. He waited until the front door closed to move toward his ex-wife. Julie crossed her legs, reclining on the couch with her second glass of mimosa.

"Answer me, damnit?" he snapped, his voice raising a tad.

Julie's eyes widened at his tone. "Why do you assume I said anything to her?"

"I know you upset her somehow."

"I don't understand you, Robert." Julie shook her head. "I don't understand you at all."

"Elaborate."

"Of all the women in the world, why her?"

"Stop beating around the bush, Julie. Whatever's on your mind, just get it out."

Julie smirked. "I know you're fucking Belinda's best friend, Robert. Crawford saw you at the Hamptons last weekend. Business trip, my ass. You took her to our vacation home, didn't you?"

"Our vacation home? We're divorced, Julie, or have you forgotten?"

"Only on paper. You and I, we're bonded for life."

"I wish you'd thought of that before inviting another man into our bed."

Julie stood, moving toward him. "A grave mistake, one I regret every day."

"Right... which is why you married the man you cheated with." He brushed aside her attempt to hold his hand.

"What did you expect me to do? You left me. I didn't want to be alone."

"Bullshit." He backed away. "I'm done talking about this."

"Of course, you are. God forbid, you tolerate a decent conversation, for once. You have always left things hanging. You refused to fight for our marriage, for me, for your daughter—"

"Don't bring Belinda into this."

"Why shouldn't I? You disappeared for two years without a word. You left her for two years, Robert."

"It was a fucking mistake! Your family didn't help, either. They did everything to poison her against me, and I allowed it to get to me. I'm trying to fix it, Goddamnit. Don't judge me, Julie. I love my daughter. Don't you ever assume otherwise."

"You have a funny way of showing it. Her best friend, Robert. That's really low."

Rob gritted his teeth. "Are you going to tell Belinda?"

"Tell Belinda?" Julie let out a dull laugh. "Are you insane? Why would I ruin her life? She needs a selfless parent in her life, Robert."

"That's unfair of you to say."

"Take a deep look inside and tell me whether it's true." Julie moved to the minibar. This time, she poured a single glass of whiskey.

Rob shook his head with a scoff. "I thought you quit that disgusting habit."

"I guess old habits die hard," Julie smirked, taking a sip.

A moment of silence settled between them. Rob regarded his ex-wife, trying to connect this woman to the sweet girl he met in college. He loved the old Julie. She wasn't the typical rich, spoiled girl. Sure, her family had money, but she was so down-to-earth, so simple. It was so easy to fall in love with her.

Everything changed when they had Belinda. They were too young, barely out of college. Rob had just gotten an entry-level job in an investment firm. He had no money to take care of a child. It was easy to fall into the safety net provided by the Bancrofts, but that also meant sacrificing a part of himself. For a while, he gave into that sacrifice, but before long, he became a lost cause. He didn't fit into their world. Julie's friends constantly reminded him of that fact.

Julie changed overnight, going from the sweet girl he loved to a woman obsessed with appearances. She wanted to compensate for disappointing her parents, but it made her just like them; snobby, mean and completely out of touch. Still, he loved her. He wanted their marriage to work.

It didn't take long for Mr. Bancroft to notice how business-savvy he was, and he offered him a cushy job at the head of his investment firm. Rob already had his sight on launching his startup. He wanted to be his own boss, not ruled by the Bancroft's iron fist. His rejection triggered the bitterness that led to their bitter divorce. It wasn't only Julie's cheating that made him leave. Even without the Bancroft's direct influence, he still felt stifled. He wanted no connection to them. For two years, it included Belinda. It was a decision he would always regret.

"Do you love her?" Julie asked, breaking into his thoughts.

Rob stared at her, blankly, until she scoffed.

"Laura. Do you love her?" Julie asked again, staring directly at him.

He turned away from her, staring out the window. The flutters in his stomach made him take a deep breath. *No, this can't be happening.*

"It will never work you know," Julie remarked. "You'll hurt Belinda, and not only that, but you'll hurt Laura too. You never know how to be grounded, Robert. Nothing was ever good enough for you. Nothing will get in between you and your stupid pride. Soon, you'll feel tied down, and eventually you'll leave, just like you always do."

Rob moved to grab his jacket. "Stay out of my life, Julie, that's all I ask."

As he walked to the front door, Julie called out, "Keep running Robert. You'll never change."

"LAURA, LET ME IN."

Rob knocked on the door for the sixth time, but there was no reply. He leaned his ear to the door, listening for movement in Laura's apartment. She was inside, he was sure of it. He didn't blame her for not wanting to let him in. The disaster in the Hamptons still left a bitter taste in his mouth. Add that to Julie knowing of their affair.

A soft click came from across the hall and Mrs. Kadinsky appeared, looking concerned. "Do you need help, dear?" she asked.

"No, thanks," he replied, rapping the door again.

"Have you tried calling her? I have her number here," she offered.

"No, thank you," he said again.

He was about to knock again when the door flew open, and he met Laura's dark glare. "What do you want?"

I want you, was his first thought. "I came to check if you're okay," were the words that left his mouth.

"Why do you care?"

Rob glanced behind him. Mrs. Kadinsky still stood by her apartment door. "Can you let me in?"

Laura huffed, then stepped aside. "You have five minutes. That's all I'm willing to spare."

Rob ran his fingers through his hair, releasing a sigh as Laura stood before him, her arms crossed against her chest. The action bunched her breasts, giving him a peek of her cleavage. He shifted his gaze, staring at her legs instead.

Big mistake.

His filthy mind wandered, evoking images of them wrapped around his waist, her eyes dark with need as he thrusted inside her. An electric tingle ran through him, his body humming. The apartment was too small. Too intimate. There were too many memories, especially on that cozy bed. He shouldn't have come.

"Four minutes, Rob. I mean it."

He sighed again, pushing the need away. "What did Julie say to you?"

"Besides revealing she knows about us? Apparently, I am a homewrecker, too. Apparently, you're still her husband."

"That's so far from the truth. I'm sorry that happened to you. I shouldn't have brought you to the Hamptons or taken you out in public. That was my error, and it won't happen again."

"You've already made that clear, Rob. No need to double-down now."

Rob took in her stiff demeanor, the tightness of her lips. "You're mad at me."

"No shit, Sherlock." She rolled her eyes. "Are you done?"

"Listen, Laura, what happened in the Hamptons—"

"Will stay in the Hamptons because I don't want to talk about it. Ever." She turned, heading to the front door. "It's time for you to leave."

"We need to talk about it, to set the record straight. Besides, we need to be on the same page if Belinda finds out."

"There's no need to set the record straight. We weren't a thing. You established that from the start. Plus, I'm too young, too immature, right?" She raised a brow at him.

"I-." Rob sighed as he trailed off.

"Go please," she said, crossing her arms.

"I'm not leaving until we have a proper conversation," he firmly said.

"Funny. Normally that would be the last thing you wanted."

He sighed heavily. "Laura, I'm trying."

She scoffed as she shook her head. "I'm tired of your hot and cold behavior, Rob. This minute you want me and the next you can't even stand to look at me. I get that all you wanted was the sex, but I can't be going back and forth with you and hurting myself in the process. You've made it clear that this can't be anything else. Why are you here?"

"Laura, don't just stand there and pretend like you don't know how complicated this is."

She swallowed. "And that's why I'm leaving you with your choice. You're free to go, do whatever you want, but I'm so tired of taking crap from people, from running behind everyone. I'm tired of getting my heart broken over and over again when I know I don't deserve it." Her voice slightly broke.

Rob swallowed visibly. "I never meant to hurt you, and I'm so sorry, but it was hard to know whether or not your feelings were genuine when I was nothing more than a rebound to you. You're not over your ex Laura and its even hard for me to think long term with you, knowing that Adam is still at the forefront."

Laura's eyes widened. "What?"

"You're not over him and you don't have to admit it to me, but I know. And even if this was to be more than what it is, it wouldn't be fair to either of us."

Laura blinked a couple times, wanting to keep the tears at bay. "I- I've never felt this way about Adam, ever. And yes, in the beginning, I wanted a distraction in Rome, but it was more than just the sex. I was hurt by what Adam did but I wasn't using you," her voice cracked.

Rob said nothing for a second.

"And you stand there accusing me of not being over Adam, when it looks like you're not even over your ex-wife," she lashed back at him.

Rob's brows furrowed. "What?" he asked.

"You still have all this pent-up anger. You don't talk about what happened."

Rob gritted his teeth as the paced the floor, flashing Laura a firm look. "Julie is my ex-wife and the mother of my child; that's all she is. There isn't a single bone in my body that still has feelings for her and I'll always be angry at her for what she put Belinda through. She didn't deserve to see that and she shouldn't have brought a man in our house knowing that our daughter would walk in at any minute. So yes, I'll always resent her for that, but saying I still have feelings for her is too great of a stretch, Laura."

Laura swallowed as their gazes met. The fire in his eyes matched hers.

"We just won't work, will we?" she said, her voice gone softer.

Rob clenched his teeth and waited a beat. He wanted so much to tell her that he wanted them to, but the logical thing to do would be to leave it as things were. They would both be fine in the end and that was what he began to tell himself. They were good for a time.

"I'm sorry," he said.

She nodded slowly as she moved towards the door and pulled it open for him. Rob paused before he moved towards the door and stopped in front of her.

"I wish things were different, Laura."

Her eyes glistened. "Me too."

With that, Rob left. Laura closed the door behind him, her back braced against the hard surface. Her lips quivered and as much as she tried to hold back, she couldn't help the tidal wave of emotions that crashed into her, opening the flood gates. She choked out a sob and slid down the door, settling on the floor with her knees drawn to her chest. Pulling herself into a ball, she cried her eyes out, her heart breaking ten times over.

Chapter 15

If only I could turn back time... Sniffling, she wiped her face. *Rob doesn't deserve my tears. I'm done pining after him. I'm done running after men who don't want to be with me.* But it was harder than what she's ever imagined.

For what seemed like hours later, her cell phone shrilled with the ring tone she'd set for Belinda, and she contemplated whether to answer. What if Julie told her the truth? Could she face her best friend's anger right now?

Remembering Belinda's resilience, Laura peeled herself from the floor and went to get her phone. She pressed the answer button with a sigh. "Hey Belinda, what's up?"

"What's up? My bachelorette party is in a few hours, or have you forgotten?"

"I haven't." *I'm just trying to convince myself to go.*

"Good, because it's my last weekend as a single woman. I want to get off the market with a bang!"

"Do I even want to know what that means?"

Belinda giggled. "I want to let my hair down and get naughty. Really naughty."

"On a scale of one to ten, how naughty?"

"I'm talking strippers. Male, female, I don't care. The dirtier, the better."

"Somehow, I don't think Julie would approve."

"Pssh. Mom's not coming, anyway."

Laura's brows lifted. "How come?"

"We just had a little fight."

"Really?" Laura asked, her stomach dipping. "About what?"

147

"She's been acting weird since yesterday. I overheard her on the phone with her best friend, talking about a homewrecker being invited to my wedding. When I asked who it was, she iced me out. Today, she confirmed that Crawford's coming to the wedding, although I specifically asked her not to invite him. It's like she's trying to drive me insane, like I'm not already stressed. God, I hate this!"

Laura closed her eyes, panic rising like bile in her throat. If Julie mentioned the affair to Liz, there was no doubt the secret wouldn't remain hidden for much longer. Plus, Crawford would be at the wedding; what if his mouth slipped to the wrong person?

Now was the time to come clean before Belinda heard from someone else. Her affair with Rob was over, anyway. Taking a deep breath, she plunged on, "Belinda I need to tell you—"

"That's the doorbell, Laura. My stylist's here. See you at the party, okay?"

"Can it wait for a minute? I really need to—"

"No time! We can talk all we want tomorrow. Don't be late. Bye!"

LAURA GAVE THE DOORMAN a polite smile as she walked through the door that led to the private lounge and Belinda's party. As usual, the setting left her feeling out of place, but like always, she put her insecurities aside, determined to support her best friend. The event planner clearly went all out with decorating the intimate space, but the raunchy theme was very unlike Belinda. What the hell did her best friend have planned for tonight?

A scantily clad server approached, handing her a cocktail with a penis-shaped straw. She relaxed, taking a sip before moving into the room. The women were mostly Belinda's friends from her childhood days and a few from college. She greeted the ones she knew before sitting alone on a loveseat. At the front of the room was a huge gold chair and a banner hanging overhead with the words, 'Same Penis Forever'. Red and gold arch balloons adorned each side.

The ladies cheered when Belinda sauntered in with a flourish, her slender frame enhanced by the skimpy dress. Laura's eyes narrowed on her face to the emptiness in her eyes. Her smile wasn't real. She also noticed Belinda didn't glance her way.

What's going on, Belinda? Do you know about me and Rob's affair?

There was no time to worry about her little secret because the festivities began. Laura's eyes widened as a handful of male strippers descended on the room, giving the guests an erotic show that would make a prostitute blush. The biggest, sexiest one zoned in on Belinda, spreading her on a makeshift bed and licking his way up her thighs. Laura cringed and turned away, too shocked to look any longer. This wasn't like Belinda. Her best friend would never act that way, not even for her bachelorette party.

The excitement soon died down, and guests mingled. Laura bee-lined for Belinda at once. "You okay?" she asked, taking in Belinda's heaving chest and the wisps of hair plastered to her forehead. She was still recovering from the encounter.

She fanned herself with a happy gasp. "Of course. I'm having a ball."

"Belinda, come on. Cut the façade. You're talking to me, remember? I know when something's not right."

Belinda's eyes dropped, and the cheerfulness evaporated. She moved away from the crowd, taking Laura with her. "Promise me you won't say a word to anyone."

"Ok... what is it?"

"It's Henry. He's seeing someone else."

Laura gasped. "What? Are you sure?"

Belinda nodded, her eyes glassy with unshed tears. "I'm positive."

"How did you find out?"

"Remember the fight we had a few weeks ago? He went to see her and turned off his phone while they were together. She's a model who lives in L.A."

"Oh, my God, Belinda... I don't know what to say. I'm so sorry. Are you sure about the wedding, though?"

Belinda nodded. "I have to marry him. There's no other option, not with the wedding only a day away."

"No, you don't. Belinda, once a cheater, always a cheater. Isn't that what they always say?"

"You're not from my world, Laura," Belinda said with a huff. "It's not as easy as you believe. There are expectations I need to meet."

"What about your happiness? Isn't it more important than what your family want?"

Belinda dabbed her eyes with the napkin. "I don't expect you to understand, so let's agree to disagree."

"You're right. I don't understand your world." *I dodged a bullet with Adam, for sure.*

She couldn't help feeling pity for Belinda, though. Her best friend had more money she could spend in this lifetime, but the misery cancelled all her wealth. *I'd rather be broke and happy with my life than wealthy and going through hell.*

A woman cut into their conversation, stealing Belinda away. With no one left to talk to, Laura made her way to the ladies' room, and she was almost there when she heard her name. She doubled back, stopping outside the room where the voices came.

"... charity case," a woman said, and Laura recognized Belinda's cousin's voice. "I don't know why Belinda keeps her around. She's like a stray dog looking for a bone."

"Oh, my God Gina. That's so harsh," Amy, Belinda's bridesmaid said with a giggle.

"Oh, please. I'm saying what everyone's afraid to say out loud. She doesn't belong in our circle. I hate how Belinda's trying to make her fit in."

"An impossible task, if you ask me. Did you see her outfit? I wouldn't be surprised if she got it off the sale rack at Ross," another woman chimed in. Belinda's high school friend, Anna. Laura leaned against the wall, her face burning with shame.

She was about to move off when Gina said, "Did you hear about her fight with Adam?"

"Oh, my God, yes. It's so embarrassing that I'm even associated with her. Imagine having to stand beside her at the wedding," Amy replied. "I'm so not looking forward to it."

Gina scoffed. "I can't believe she thought Adam would marry her someday. We all knew she was a placeholder. I don't know why she was surprised when he left her."

"Imagine breaking up with your lover while on your way to get married. So wrong!"

"And so scandalous!" Gina chuckled. "We all knew it would come to this. Even Belinda."

Wait... what? Belinda knew?

An ice-like sensation surged through Laura's veins, rendering her to shock. She backed away from the door, returning to the party, her heart crashing against her chest. Hearing the girls' slander hurt, but it was nothing compared to Belinda's betrayal. *How could she do this to me?*

She found Belinda at the bar, throwing back a shot. "We need to talk."

Belinda blew a breath, signaling to the bartender to pour another shot. "Not now, Laura."

"Why didn't you tell me about Victoria?"

Belinda stiffened, her guilty expression erasing Laura's lingering doubt. "Oh, my God. Who told you?"

"Does it matter? If what I heard is true, then it also means you befriended me out of pity. Did you?"

Belinda closed her eyes with a head shake. "Laura—"

"Forget it. I don't need your response." Lifting her purse from the bar counter, she stormed out, the double doors slamming shut behind her. It wasn't until she reached the curb that her conscience chipped in.

I'm a hypocrite. Belinda wasn't the only one carrying a secret. In fact, what I did was so much worse.

With a loud, conceding breath, she made a U-turn. Belinda still sat at the bar, sobbing as she took another shot. Laura's chest tightened with remorse. Determined to make it right, she moved forward.

"Hey."

Belinda whipped around with a tear-streak face; her expression relieved as she wrapped her arms around Laura. "Oh, Laura... you came back!"

"I had to. I'm sorry for losing my temper," Belinda replied, returning the hug.

"No... it's okay. I deserve it. I should have been honest from the start. Laura, you're not a charity case. Our friendship wasn't formed out of pity. Screw whatever Gina said. She's just jealous because you're my maid of honor, not her."

Laura nodded, her chin bouncing on Belinda's shoulder. "Deep down, I didn't believe it, anyway."

"You're the best friend anyone could ask for. I wouldn't trade you for the world. You're kind, forgiving, honest... I'm so happy you're in my life, Laura. I mean it."

"Aww, Belinda." Laura tightened her arms around Belinda, tears forming in her eyes. She didn't deserve Belinda's praise. If only Belinda knew the secret she kept close to her chest.

Tell her. Tell her now.

She eased off Belinda, staring into her best friend's weary face. "Belinda, I..."

I slept with your dad. Not just once, or twice. In fact, I've fallen in love with him, too.

Why can't I get the words out?

"I know, sweetie." Belinda squeezed her arm. "I love you too."

Laura sighed. *This isn't the best place or time. In fact, I can't think of any suitable time. There's no way I can break my best friend's heart.*

Chapter 16

"Loosen up, Daddy."

Rob forced a smile, taking in his beautiful daughter—his beautiful princess. In half an hour, she would be someone's wife. Seeing her all dolled up in the stunning ball gown brought reality home. She wasn't his little girl anymore. "I am loose," he replied.

"No, you're tense, and it's making me nervous. Is there something bothering you?"

"No, I'm quite fine." The lie easily slipped from his lips, and he hoped it was enough to placate her. "How about you? Are you ready to start your new life as Henry's wife?"

"As ready as I'll ever be, I guess," Belinda replied, letting out a soft breath.

Rob scrutinized her face, taking in the emptiness in her eyes, the tightness of her lips. "Are you sure about that?"

She nodded, blinking furiously.

"Honey, talk to me. Is everything okay?"

A tear ran down Belinda's cheek, and she nodded again. "I'm fine, Dad, just wedding jitters."

"Positive?"

Belinda opened her mouth as Julie sauntered over to them, lashing Rob with a hard stare. "Of course, she's sure. Come on, honey, it's time to make me the happiest mother alive."

"At the sacrifice of *her* happiness, am I right?"

"Don't start, Rob. It's your daughter's wedding day. I don't need you spoiling things for her."

"That's not what I'm—never mind." There was no use arguing with Julie, especially when it was Belinda's big day. He offered his arm and

Belinda took it, the forced smile plastered on her face. His instincts chipped in. They were almost at the door when he took her shoulders, staring earnestly at her. "Belinda don't do this. Please, call off the wedding."

Belinda gasped, her eyes watering once more. "Dad—"

"For God's sake, Rob," Julie cut in, roughly prying them apart. "Leave her alone. You have a knack for ruining things, but today won't be one of them. If you don't want to walk your daughter down the aisle, I will."

Rob scoffed. "Are you blind? Isn't it obvious she doesn't want to marry this guy?"

"What's obvious is you trying to mess with her head. She loves Henry. I'm sure she's dying to meet him at the altar, aren't you, Belinda?" Julie asked, regarding her daughter.

"Uh..." Belinda began, her expression hesitant.

Julie gave her a direct stare. "Don't tell me you're having second thoughts. You owe me, Belinda."

"You're such a manipulative bitch," Rob blurted, frustrated. "She owes you nothing, Julie. The divorce wasn't her fault. She made the right decision by telling me, stop hanging it over her head."

"Is that what I'm doing, or am I ensuring our daughter is secured by another powerful family for life?

"Anything for an image, right? Screw happiness. If Henry's so great, why the fuck don't you marry him? Oh, I forgot, you're already screwing a boy toy."

"You're one to talk, you cradle robber," Julie said, whirling on him. "I know your secret, Robert, don't you forget. Get out of our way, or I'll tell Belinda all about your disgusting sin."

The determination in Julie's eyes dropped a dilemma onto his lap. Should he risk exposing his affair to convince his daughter not to make this grave mistake? The affair was over; would Belinda forgive him, anyway?

"Yes, I thought so," Julie said haughtily when he made no move. She took Belinda's arm. "Come on, honey, the guests must be wondering where we are."

"Wait a minute." Belinda tugged her arm from Julie's with a deep frown. "What sin is she talking about, Dad?"

"It's nothing," he replied as a knock sounded. Laura's face appeared a moment later, the sight rendering him to shock, erasing the frustration and replacing it with awe. She was stunning in that red dress, her hair hanging loosely around her shoulders. His pulse fluttered. The air left the room. He took a deep breath, but it was no use. The long-forgotten emotion swirled inside him. He closed his eyes, pushing it away.

"What is it?" Julie snapped.

Laura's eyes narrowed. "The priest seems a bit impatient, so I came to check if Belinda's okay."

"She's obviously fine, Laura. Why don't you try being useful for once in your life and hold her train?" Julie replied, still snapping.

"Don't talk to Laura like that," Rob cut in. "Be an asshole to someone else, not her."

Julie cocked her head, smirking. "What, afraid I'll hurt your little girlfriend's feelings? She's bold enough to sleep with you. I'm sure she can handle my mouth."

Fuck.

Belinda's eyes widened. Laura covered her mouth. Julie swore, slapping her forehead. Rob suspected she was more upset about losing her leverage than hurting Belinda.

"What did you just say?" Belinda asked Julie, her eyes darting from Rob to Laura, whose gaze locked to the floor.

"Honey, can we talk about this later? We don't want to keep the guests waiting any longer, do we?"

"I don't care about the guests!" Belinda screamed. "I don't care about Henry either. He can go marry that slut he's been fucking for all I care."

"Belinda!" Julie exclaimed.

"What? Henry's been sleeping with someone else?" Rob thundered.

Belinda rounded on him. "Don't change the subject, Dad. What is mom talking about? Have you been sleeping with my best friend?"

Rob glanced at Laura still staring at the floor, fiddling with her dress. There was no denying the truth. "Yes."

"Oh, my God." Belinda moaned, directing her attention to Laura. "I can't believe this..."

Laura lifted her gaze, giving Belinda a pleading stare. "I'm so sorry, Belinda. I never meant to hurt you, I swear—"

"How long has this been going on?" Belinda asked.

"There's nothing going on, Belinda," Rob spoke up. "It was just a fling. It meant nothing. I certainly wasn't trying to hurt you. Laura and I met in Rome and—"

"In Rome?" Belinda gasped, twisting to Laura. "*My dad* was the guy you've been gushing over. Are you fucking kidding me?"

Laura didn't reply. Her eyes were trained on Rob, the hurt clear within them. Rob grimaced, remembering what he just said. It wasn't true. Their affair wasn't just a random fling. Laura wasn't like the other women he'd been with. She had gotten deep under his skin and stayed there.

The tears spilled down her cheeks as she backed out of the room. He didn't know if her tears were for Belinda or his ill-timed words. Whatever it was, he hated seeing her fall apart like this. The last thing he wanted to do was hurt her...again.

"I'm really sorry, Belinda. I need to go." Her sobs echoed down the hallway, clashing with the clicking of her heels as she beat a hasty retreat.

Rob blew out a harsh breath, running his fingers through his hair. Damn it. Damn it all to hell.

"How could you do this to me, Daddy?" Belinda asked, tearing up. "She's my best friend, the only genuine friend I have in this world. There were plenty of other women out there. Why her?"

"Genuine friend, my ass. She was only using you for a way into our circle, and now she's got it." Julie scoffed, gesturing to Rob.

"Mom, just shut it, please." Belinda ignored Julie's loud gasp, directing her attention to Rob. "Why her, Dad?"

Rob swallowed. "She makes me feel alive, Belinda. Happy. Free. Yes, she makes me feel free, like my old self again." he replied. The words left him a rush, leaving him with an awareness that stole his breath. "When we met in Rome we had the best time and I swear, we didn't each other. I didn't know she was your best friend, but we connected and I'm sorry sweetheart, but I never meant to hurt you."

"Oh, my God," Belinda whispered, her trembling hands cupping her cheek. "You're in love with her."

Rob closed his eyes with a sigh. There was no denying the obvious. "Yes."

"This is bullshit, Rob. She's just a child," Julie spoke up.

"Whatever, Mom. Your opinion isn't needed right now," Belinda said, glaring at her.

Julie gasped, clutching her pearls. "How dare you speak to me that way? I am your mother, damn it!"

Belinda sighed, her expression shuttering. "Mom, I need to speak with my father, alone. Please, see yourself out. You can let the guests know there won't be a wedding today."

"You'll regret this, I swear to God."

"The only thing I regret is letting you encourage me to stay with Henry after I found out he was seeing someone else. I'm done being your yes girl. Find another puppet, Mom. I'm done."

"Well, I never!" Julie stared at Belinda like she'd never seen her before.

"You heard her, Julie," Rob said with a smirk. "Don't let the door hit you on the way out."

"Fine. I'm done. You both deserve each other." She marched out, the door slamming after her.

"Wipe that smirk off your face, Dad. I'm still mad at you," Belinda said, crossing her arms. "Why didn't you tell me?"

Rob's expression sobered. "How could I, Belinda?"

"By opening your mouth and saying the words."

"I couldn't. I was too busy trying not to lose control." *I failed miserably, anyway.*

"How did that work out?"

"I don't want to talk about the details, Belinda. It feels weird. I didn't want to hurt you, and I'm sorry I did. Please forgive me."

Belinda brushed his comment aside with a sweep of her hand. "Why does it feel weird?"

"Isn't it obvious? It's wrong."

"What's wrong about it?"

"She's old enough to be my kid."

"But she's not your kid. I am, and I'm letting you know I'm okay." She moved towards him, taking his hands. "I would have been mad if you only wanted sex, but it's clear you have feelings for her. You have my blessing, Dad."

His brows lifted. "Do you mean that, or are you messing with me?"

"Of course, I do. I never mess around with love. Just don't break her heart. It's very fragile."

Rob groaned. "I think it's too late for that."

"What do you mean?"

"Didn't you hear what I said earlier? I told you the affair meant nothing."

"Oh, that." She shrugged. "I'm sure she'll understand once you explain. You need to go see her, Dad."

"Fine. I will."

"Tell her I'm not mad anymore, okay? I'll talk to her tomorrow."

"Wait," Rob said as Belinda made for the exit. "Forget about me for a moment. Are you okay?"

"I'm fine, Dad," she replied with a genuine smile. "I'm relieved. For the first time in months, I'll go to bed not worrying if Henry's with another woman."

"I'm glad you've come to your senses. Saved me the trouble of beating the shit out of that cheating asshole."

Belinda chuckled. "I just might need you to deliver on that offer, anyway."

"Don't tempt me, please. Do you want me to drop you home?"

"No, I'm fine. I'll call my driver. Go get Laura."

He was already through the door, his heart in his throat, hoping it wasn't too late.

Chapter 17

The door slammed behind Laura as she stormed into her apartment, still overcome with tears. She collapsed onto the bed, curling into a ball, her body racking from her emotional breakdown. Hearing the words from Rob's mouth was like a knife in her heart. *It was just an affair. It meant nothing.*

God, make this pain go away. Please.

She shouldn't have been mad. Didn't Rob make it clear what they had was just a fling? Hadn't he been honest from the start? Plus, they cleared things up the other day – decided that them not seeing each other was for the better.

It hurt to hear him deny her in front of Julie and Belinda. *Oh, Belinda...*

She burst in a fresh wave of tears, remembering the betrayal on her best friend's face. Their friendship would never rebound from this. It was over. She'd lost the only friend, and for what, a man who would never return her love? Too late, she realized it wasn't worth it. He wasn't worth losing her friend.

He's not worth my tears, either.

Getting out of bed, she undressed and showered, hoping it would lighten her mood. It didn't. She slipped on an old T-shirt and curled up on the couch with her laptop, checking her email. She'd sent several art submissions online, hoping to get her artwork in a gallery. If any luck, she would have several doors opened for her. She needed a small victory after that disaster today.

There was nothing.

With a heavy heart, she shut the laptop and closed her eyes. *What did I do in my past life to deserve this? Can't I win, for once?*

She was about to turn on the TV when the doorbell rang. *Not Mrs. Kadinsky again,* she thought. Her inquisitive neighbor had already rung twice after Laura rushed by her earlier in tears. While she usually welcomed Mrs. Kadinsky's nurturing attention, she wasn't in the mood to explain her anguish. It was too hurtful. Too raw. She got up anyway, prepared to lie about a headache to get Mrs. Kadinsky off her back. Rob's contrite expression was the last thing she expected after opening the door. Her reflexes kicked in. With a click of her tongue, she pushed the door, but Rob stuck out his foot to stop it from closing.

"Laura—"

"Don't you dare say my name. Get your foot out the door so I can close it."

"I can't do that." He lashed her with a pleading stare that made her pulse race. "Let me in, Laura. Please."

"No. If you have something to say, there's plenty of space in the hallway. I don't want you in my apartment." Especially when her emotions were on an incline. She hated this weakness for him.

Rob huffed. "Fine."

Her fingers curled around the edge of the door, watching as he backed into the hallway. His eyes never left her. She couldn't look away. The temptation to let him in increased with each passing minute.

No, Laura. Be strong.

"I'm sorry, Laura," he began. "What I said in that room... I never meant to hurt you."

Laura shrugged, arranging a casual expression. "Whatever. I shouldn't have been surprised or hurt. You've made it clear there's no future for us. I got the message, Rob, loud and clear this time."

"What I'm saying is—"

"I get it, okay? I'm not from your world. I don't belong on your arm when you're bumping shoulders with the rich and entitled. I'm nothing but a secret pity fuck."

"That's nowhere near the truth, Laura—"

"I don't care! Look, I've already moved on. In fact, I have a date tonight that I'm trying to prepare for. So, if there's nothing else, goodbye."

Rob's expression darkened, and he gave her a quick nod. "Have a great life, Laura. I mean it." Without waiting for a reply, he spun on his heels, leaving Laura in another flood of tears.

"THANK YOU FOR COMING," Laura said to Belinda as her best friend took her seat in the fast casual restaurant she agreed to meet for their lunch date. Well, she hoped Belinda was still her best friend. They hadn't spoken since the non-wedding last week.

"Of course." Belinda shot her a smile. "I'm sorry about being MIA all week. I just needed to get away and clear my head. Henry has been calling me non-stop, begging for another chance. I had to turn my phone off."

"Trust me, I understand how necessary that was. How are you feeling, anyway?"

"Like I dodged a freaking bullet..." Belinda giggled. "I'm laughing now, but it wasn't so funny when I found out. I was devastated. Now, I'm so grateful. I wasn't ready to be anyone's wife."

"Is your mom still mad at you?"

Belinda rolled her eyes. "Ugh. She'll get over it. Right now, she's busy handling the news about Crawford and that Victoria Secret model. Dad says it's karma. Sadly, I agree."

"I imagine how vindicated he must feel right now. I can't wait for that feeling, too."

"Adam will get his, believe me. There's a rumor he's not happy in his marriage. I don't know if it's true, but I hope so. Asshole."

"Either way, I'm glad he broke up with me. It's the best decision he made."

"Right, because you're happier without him."

"One hundred percent."

Belinda smiled. "Thanks for looking out for me. You were the only one who encouraged me to leave Henry, the only one who realized how unhappy I was. I love you, Laura."

"I love you, too," Laura replied, tearing up. "I almost went crazy thinking you were mad at me."

"I'm still mad at you, but not for what you think. You should have been honest with me, Laura. Best friends tell each other everything."

"I know, but don't you realize how awkward it was for me?"

Belinda smiled. "Like I told Dad, you have my blessing. I mean, it's weird imagining you and my father together, but I'll get used to it. What matters is how happy you are with each other."

Laura placed her fork on the table. "You're confusing me."

"How?"

"You gave us your blessing? What does that mean?"

It was Belinda's turn to frown. "Didn't Dad tell you? I was mad because I thought you were just a notch on his belt, but he loves you. I can't stand in the way of love, can I?"

"Wait... what?"

Rob loves me?

"Are you okay? You look pale. Hey, Laura—" Belinda reach over the table and shook her hand. "You need to breathe."

Laura gulped, taking in a huge breath, then releasing it. *He came to tell me he loved me, didn't he? I sent him away. Oh, my God.* She dipped in her purse for her phone.

"What are you doing?" Belinda asked.

"I'm calling him."

"Did something happen with you two? He's on a business trip to Europe. I thought you knew that." She clicked her tongue. "You didn't talk to him, did you?"

"He came to the apartment, but I sent him away. I told him I was seeing someone else, Belinda. I didn't know— oh, my God…"

"Oh no…I'm sure it will be fine, don't worry."

There was no way to stop worrying, though. What if she'd missed that window? What if she lost Rob for good?

Chapter 18

"I can't believe this. Are you for real?"

Laura switched the phone to her other ear, doing a little jig in the center of her living room. The call from Antonio was the last she expected after waking this morning with the heaviness that had been with her all week. *How did he even get my number, anyway? It's hard to believe it came from Rob.* He hadn't contacted her all week, nor had he returned her calls or text messages. She had resigned herself to the reality that they were truly over. Her heart hadn't gotten the message yet, though.

Antonio chuckled on the other end. "I am for real, Belinda. I'd like to have your work displayed in my New York gallery when it launches in September."

"But... you haven't seen my work. How do you know if they are good enough?"

"Rob's seen them, and he vouches for their quality. I trust his judgement. Still, I'd like samples of them delivered to me, so we can discuss their placement in the gallery."

"Of course. Oh, my God. This is surreal. I can't thank you enough."

"Thank Rob. He's been on my case all week, reminding me to call you. I don't know what you've done to him, but he's quite taken with you."

Laura's heart lurched, confusion reigning supreme. *He did this for me. Why, when he hasn't been taking my calls? It makes no sense. I need to know why. I need to see him.*

She ended the call with Antonio and emailed the samples to him, then took a quick shower. According to Belinda's updates, Rob had returned to New York a few days ago. Despite her best friend's blessing, it felt weird asking Belinda for his home address, so she opted to visit his office instead. He spent most of his time there, anyway. Fingers crossed; he wouldn't throw her out.

LAURA GAVE THE FRONT desk security guard a smile as he handed her the access pass and she listened to his directions to Rob's office. The elevator ride up felt like forever, and she took nervous steps toward the glass doors. It opened before she got there and Rob emerged, not surprised to see her. He wasn't happy, either. His dark gaze took her in as she approached, her heart lodged in her throat.

"Hi," he greeted as she stopped before him.

"Hi." Every rehearsed thought disappeared, leaving her at a loss for words. She was grateful when he gestured for her to enter, and she did so quickly, stepping into a cozy office space. The spectacular view made her forget why she came but only for a moment. Rob's presence behind her was an instant reminder, forcing her to turn around. His expression said nothing, as usual.

"Thank you for calling Antonio," she began. "I appreciate it, more than I can ever show."

Rob shook his head. "I didn't do it for a thank you, Laura. You're a talented young woman. The world needs to see your work."

"Was that your only reason?"

His brows furrowed. "Did I need another reason? Isn't your talent enough?"

"I thought it was an olive branch; that you wanted to be with me."

His frown darkened, and he moved to his desk. "Does it matter? Aren't you seeing someone else?"

"What? No. I lied about having a date that night. I didn't know—" She inhaled, hoping she wasn't about to put her foot in her mouth. "I didn't know you loved me."

Rob looked up from his computer. For the first time, she saw the emotion on his face. He scoffed, returning his gaze to the screen. "I don't play games, Laura. Been there, done that."

In other words, you don't want to be with me. Laura took the hint, pivoting and heading to the exit. His grip on her arm brought her to a halt before she got there. He pulled her against him, tilting her chin, giving her the most intense stare. "Don't you ever fuck with my head like that, Laura. Never again."

"I promise," she whispered, her stomach clenching with need. She moaned with relief when their lips met, and she immediately surrendered to the delicious strokes of his tongue. She had been aching for this, for him, and from the way he ate her mouth, the feeling was mutual.

Rob broke the kiss, pressing his forehead to hers. "In case that kiss didn't make it clear, I love you, Laura. You make me feel more alive than I've been for years. I'd be a fool to let this go."

"Oh Rob," she breathed, joy filling her. *Please let this not be a dream.*

"I want to date you, to wake up to you each morning. Hell, I'd love to marry you someday." He clasped her cheeks. "I've also never been more scared in my life because with you, I have no control."

"I'm scared, too, Rob, but I'd rather be scared than live without you."

"Me, too, Laura." He planted a gentle kiss on her forehead. "Let's take those baby steps together, shall we?"

"I'd love that," she replied, breaking into a smile.

"You, me and dinner tonight, how does that sound?"

"Add some steamy make-up sex to the list and I'm all in."

Rob grinned, pulling her close once more. "You've got it."

"I love you," she said and they shared a kiss.

KNOW ABOUT MY 10 BOOKS for 1 MEGA DEAL?

Only $2.99 or Free for KU & Prime Members for my 10 Books Collection

Each book is sold for $2.99 individually. A no-brainer deal. Grab yours.

10 BOOKS COLLECTION[1]

2

CLICK HERE TO DOWNLOAD[3]

AN EXTRA STEAMY 10 BOOKS BOX SET

OVER 1,000 PAGES

Get the first 10 stories in this series in one quick download.

These stories are insta-love, fast paced standalones that can be read in any order. All are extremely steamy and have a HEA ending.

Some of the themes are age-gap/older man younger woman romance, enemies to lovers, bully romance, grumpy boss, huge mountain man and more ...

List of stories inside:

1. Daddy's Taboo Family-Friend.

---

2. Possessive Alpha-Daddy
3. Daddy's Bully-Heir
4. Off-Limits Coach Daddy
5. Daddy's Little Birthday Girl
6. My Roommate's Sexy Daddy
7. Huge Mountain Daddy
8. Grumpy Christmas Mountain Man
9. MC Daddy Possessive Biker
10. Big Brother's Quarterback Friend.?

Grab your copy HERE[4]

Pssst ... Do you enjoy reading full length novels? If yes, then I have some great *'insiders' info'* just for you, but keep this on the hush. This deal is only for readers who have at least read one of my books to the end, ok? Did you know you can have 8 full-length novels plus an extra steamy bonus story from me, for just **$2.99** or ***download it for free*** if you are a Kindle Unlimited or Prime Member? This amazing deal is ***over 2,100 pages***. Get this super deal below ^_^ ...

5

CLICK HERE TO GET THE DEAL[6]

A HOT, STEAMY COLLECTION OF AGE-GAP ROMANCE NOVELS.

List of novels inside are:

Heating Up the Kitchen - a reverse harem romance

Just Can't Behave - a forbidden, age-gap romance

Protection Details - a bodyguard, forbidden, age-gap romance

Getting Through the Seasons - a stepbrother's best friend, enemies to lovers

Getting Through the Seasons 2

Getting Through the Seasons 3

A Dose of Sunshine - a rockstar, enemies to lovers romance

Mr. Grumpy's Fake Ex-wife - a boss, stalker, enemies to lovers romance

A Bonus Novella - My Roommate's Daddy - an instalove, OTT, age-gap romance

All are standalones, contain no cheating and have happy-ever-after endings ♡

Don't miss out on this fantastic offer, grab your copy today.

That's a completed 3 books series, 5 full length novels and a novella inside. **CLICK HERE**[7] to download and enjoy!

Let's connect.

Get this book for **FREE**[8] when you sign up for our newsletter.

WICKEDLY STEAMY & FILTHY!

---

5. https://www.amazon.com/dp/B0B1YTNCKQ

6. https://www.amazon.com/dp/B0B1YTNCKQ

7. https://www.amazon.com/dp/B0B1YTNCKQ

8. https://dl.bookfunnel.com/51j08erf93

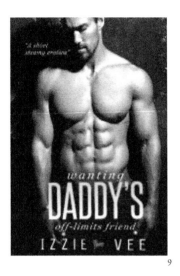

9

[CLICK HERE TO GET FOR FREE](https://dl.bookfunnel.com/51j08erf93)[10]

SAMPLE

I COULDN'T BELIEVE that I was about to head off to college and never had a sexual experience in my life. The person I considered my boyfriend in my senior years of high school was initially the person I thought I would take the big step with but later found that he only had one intention in mind, and that was to fuck the only girl in our year who was rumored to still be a virgin – me. It had hurt, and I had broken off the relationship with a few heated words thrown at him but later realized there wasn't much I wanted out of the relationship either rather than sex.

I didn't want to be a virgin anymore, so I picked the boy that had given me the most attention and decided that he was the one. Unfortunately, he wasn't and here I was, about to head off to college with my hymen intact.

If it were only based on desire alone, then my dream guy would be the one who came over to my house every now and then with all his

---

9. https://dl.bookfunnel.com/51j08erf93

10. https://dl.bookfunnel.com/51j08erf93

charm and kindness. He was the first crush I ever had, but I knew there was nothing I could make of the relationship considering he was my father's best friend.

Connor was everything I wanted in a man; he was sweet, kind, caring, incredibly handsome, and packing for his age. He taught gym at the college that I was accepted into, which made my excitement all the more profound. Dad said that Connor would be there to look out for me as he had always done, and I ... *To continue reading get your FREE DOWNLOAD HERE[11]*.

Printed in Great Britain
by Amazon

27646247R00106